CAL
STC
A SINGLE WORD

The Story of Santa Zita

By Elliot Lord

© 2011

All rights reserved

1. The servant opened his master's heavy, wooden front door to see an old peasant woman in threadbare clothes. She looked up at the servant with a face that constantly trembled from her old age. Her bony hand, covered with skin that was so fine it was almost transparent, held the hand of a young girl. The girl stood motionless, staring down at the ground in front of her as the servant frowned and tried to judge what he was presented with.

"We don't have any food. It's difficult enough trying to feed ourselves, woman," he said with an air of dismissal.

"No sir, it's not food we need," replied the old woman quickly so as not to lose her only chance to speak before he closed the door.

"Don't even dare to ask for any money," he quickly retorted. "And I don't want to see you here again."

"I haven't come to take anything, I have something to give to your master," the old woman just managed as the servant was closing the door.

He stopped for a second, then pulled it back open. "What can you possibly have to give to this household? You can barely afford to clothe yourself and your grandchild."

"She is not my grandchild," she explained with a thin voice, "her mother has just died and she wants to be of service to you."

The child continued to pay no attention to what was being said. With her long hair half-covering her face, the servant could just make out two pretty young eyes as they stared fixedly at the door. He looked her up and down with his mouth twisted in contempt as he had become used to viewing people who came to the house unannounced.

"What use is she? She's only a little girl."

"She has had a sign from God saying that she is destined to be at the mercy of a master who can use her to perform his work as he wishes."

"Well, my master is not here today, he is away on business."

"When will he return?"

"Not until next week but I'm sure he wouldn't be interested. He has enough servants here already."

"What day will he be back?"

"Next Wednesday but don't bother coming here again. We don't need anybody else."

"Thank you, sir. Goodbye."

He stood in the doorway watching as the old woman turned round. He finally saw the girl move as she took particular care to steady the frail woman and support her as they slowly walked down the path.

"Don't worry, Signora, I'm sure I can find a family that will take me," said Zita.

They carefully walked back to the old woman's tiny home and went inside. It was dark and had the same musty smell that had lingered for years since Signora Battelli had been unable to clean it properly. Zita helped her to sit down on one of only two chairs that she possessed and turned her attention to sweeping the floor.

"You shouldn't be here looking after me, my dear girl. I can't support you here."

"You don't need to do anything for me. Now that my mother is gone, God bless her, it is my duty to take care of other people. That's what she always told me. It is my penance for the poor people who spend their life in sin."

Signora Battelli sat, pensively watching Zita as she swept, then scrubbed the floor, not wavering for a second from her work. She hoped that they could find a family that needed a servant soon, as she thought it would be unjust for Zita to have to stay taking care of her. Zita's mother had used to help out here as the two families had known each other for years. Signora Battelli's only son had died young and she was resigned to grow old on her own. She knew she didn't have much time left herself but prayed that they could find a post for Zita before she became too much of a burden for her.

The days went by and Zita continued her chores in the same way, without worrying about her future. She only thought about what needed to be done at that moment. Signora Battelli felt guilty that the only thing she could offer Zita in return was somewhere to sleep but Zita always made very little of the concerns, saying that she didn't need anything except God's approval.

On the Tuesday, Zita had been helping out in the market, throwing away the rotten foods for anyone who needed it done and retuned to the house with a few vegetables and a small piece of beef as her pay. The small village of Montsegradi had no more than three thousand inhabitants and for them, life was practically the same every day. People struggled to feed themselves adequately and many of the residents would resort to cheating and stealing if they were going to prevent themselves or their children from going hungry again.

Montsegradi was relatively near to the sea but too far for anyone here to travel unless they had a horse and carriage. It was only those who owned farms who even had a horse and carriages were few and far between; a luxury for the rich families only, who were unlikely to frequent the village. This meant that fish was not a food that was easily available, and being so scarce, the price of it was too high for most people here. Most people used their small plots of land to grow a few miserable specimens of vegetables and when they were lucky enough to grow good-sized ones, they would rather sell them and use the money to buy more, low quality foods.

"We must try again at the Fatinelli's house tomorrow, dear," Signora Battelli reminded her.

"But we were told not to go there again."

"He just says that to all the beggars that go there but we are not begging for anything."

"Yes, that's true. We shall go there after I have been to the market."

Zita then went about her task to prepare some dinner for them both. She meticulously peeled the carrots and the turnip so as not to waste the slightest bit. She started the fire and boiled them with the meat in the only pot that there was in the simple little house. As she waited, Zita watched the small icon nearby as the flames illuminated it. She held her hands together and whispered her prayers for her mother and for the woman who was so kind as to let her stay so that she would have someone to devote herself to. They felt the cold wind that found its way through the holes in the walls. The house had stood there for generations and the weather had taken its toll, rendering it a crumbling building that had been patched up with stones that weren't quite big enough to fill the gaps and the mud that had been intended to hold them in had crumbled away.

The next day, after they had eaten some bread and fish for their lunch, Zita put on her best dress, which was the only one other than the one she worked in, and washed her hands carefully so make herself as presentable as possible. They walked back through the streets to the Fatinelli house and Zita had prepared herself to be more cheerful this time to try to convince the master to let her work for him.

Zita knocked on the door and the same servant opened it.

"I told you not to come here again," he said with a look of authority.

"Please excuse us, sir," said Zita as she stood with an upright posture and a hint of a smile on her face. "I only beg you to ask your master to consider letting me work for him."

"I can't, he's asleep at the moment and he doesn't like to be woken."

"I ask for nothing in return other than a place to sleep and a small amount to eat. Otherwise, I will do any work that he requires."

As Zita stood there looking innocently at her with her bright green eyes smiling at him, he found it difficult to turn them away.

"It's not a good time right now but I will tell him that you came," he said.

Just then, he heard mumbling in the room to his right. Signor Fatinelli had been disturbed by the noise at the front door and shouted out to his servant. "What's happening out there? I'm trying to sleep here, you know!"

"You'll have to excuse me but I must attend to my master," he said quickly as he closed the door.

He went into the lounge with his heart already beating quickly and bowed before his master who was lying under his blanket on the sofa.

"I told you I didn't want to be disturbed!" he grumbled. His eyes could barely be seen under the thick grey eyebrows that enhanced his frown.

"I am very sorry, sir. There is an old woman and a young girl at the front door."

"So get rid of them! I'm getting sick of beggars. I'm going to have a gate put up out there so they can't even reach the house any more."

"They are not beggars, sir. The girl is asking to become your servant. Her mother has died and she is being looked after by an old lady."

"Servant? How old is is she?"

"I don't know sir. I would guess about ten years old."

"Ten? Well, at least I wouldn't have to pay her. Are they still there?"

"I'm not sure, sir. I had to close the door and come to your service immediately."

"Well, go and see and if she's there, bring her in to me."

The servant went back to the front door and Zita had been waiting patiently with the old woman. He opened it to see again Zita's beautiful eyes smiling hopefully at him.

"Signor Fatinelli wishes to see you. Please come in."

They entered the doorway and the hall was bigger than

Signora Battelli's house in its entirety. The servant asked her to sit down on a chair there while he took Zita into the master's lounge.

Signor Fatinelli was by now sitting up on the sofa with the blanket pushed to the side. He examined Zita as she was guided through to stand before him.

"What's your name, girl?"

"Zita, your honour."

"And how old are you?"

"Twelve years old, sir."

"And what is it that you wish to offer me?"

"I would like to be your servant, sir. I do not ask for any payment but as long as I could have a bed to sleep in and some food to eat, I would be more than satisfied."

"I see, and what kind of work can you do?"

"Anything you would require, sir. I took care of my mother until she recently died. I can cook, bake, clean, and run any errands that need doing."

"Well, if you don't need any money, then I think I can take you on."

"Oh, sir, that would be a gift from God himself!"

"Paolo, show the girl to the attic and her first task will be to clear a space for her to sleep in."

They both left the room and Signor Fatinelli lay back down and went to sleep.

"Signora, he has accepted me as his servant!"

The old woman was very relieved to hear this and they went back to her home for Zita to collect her few possessions, those being her working dress and her rosary beads. She bade farewell to the woman, who was happier that Zita had her destiny decided than she was sad that she would be alone during her last days.

2. In May 1224, Zita began her new life as a maid for the Fatinelli family. Signor Fatinelli, an influential and powerful tradesman, was known for his ruthless deals and control of markets in the Republic of Lucca.. With hair that was half-grey, half-black and scraped back from his receding brow and his overbearing thick forehead, deep with lines from many years of frowning and complaining, he gave off a commanding air simply from the way he looked at people. His wily, small brown eyes were set deep under his usually lowered eyebrows and his thick moustache that covered his top lip completely helped to keep his facial expressions a secret from whoever he was talking to. He had connections with the local church of St. Frediano, with whom he diverted some of his trading profits to keep it at the seat of local government.

He was at home during Zita's first days there and he observed her behaviour as she settled in and learnt her tasks from the other staff.

Zita was provided with a small, dusty space in the attic where she had a small bed and an old, battered chest in which to keep her dress and beads. Signor Fatinelli was almost irritated when he found no indication that she was dissatisfied with her sleeping quarters. It was his intention to put her to her first test by providing her with the minimum of necessities but Zita did nothing more than methodically make her bed with utmost neatness and use her spare time to clear away the dust.

The Fatinelli home was a large building surrounded by a well-tended garden. The ground floor comprised of a drawing room at one end, and another adjoining it where Signora Fatinelli entertained her guests. This joined onto the dining room which was large enough to seat eighteen people at the impressively decorated table. Following this, a kitchen which, being almost constantly warm, was actually the room where the servants preferred to be even though it could get very crowded when friends were coming to dinner. The servants' rooms lay beyond the kitchen, with meagre rooms to accommodate the eight staff employed by the family.

Upstairs were the bedrooms which were beautiful to see, with hand-woven rugs and blankets which caught the morning sun beautifully and reflected a rich light around the rooms. The Fatinellis had three children; two boys and a girl. The oldest boy Giuseppe was sixteen and was being trained to take on a position of responsibility with his father, for whom he already worked. The girl, Beatrice, was thirteen and quite happy to be following in her mother's footsteps, learning the ways in which to dress with an air of superiority and to accompany it with similar manners. She was practising her skills on her brothers, who quite frequently tried to avoid her demeaning tone and her attempts to order them about. The youngest son, Filipe, was less interested in following his brother's and sister's footsteps and was more content to spend time in the garden, studying the plants and creatures when he was not with his friends. Although he was nine, he had a more mature perspective on life than his sister who was more interested in herself than those stupid little creatures, as she called them.

Zita was set to work in the kitchen with the head maid, Maria, who told her to peel and chop a large pile of vegetables for a dinner that the family was having for their equally affluent friends.

She sat down on a stool and got to work without as much as saying a word to anyone who passed into the kitchen.

Fatinelli was intrigued to see how she was settling in and approached the door to the kitchen, standing behind it so that he could just see Zita from behind as she took care to peel the vegetables almost as though she was sculpting them.

"How do you expect to get those finished in time for dinner?" he bellowed as he stepped in with planned surprise.

Zita barely reacted but simply turned her smiling face to him. "I'm used to doing the best I can when preparing any food, sir."

"Well, you're going to hold up the whole proceeding going

that slowly. Get a move on."

Zita nodded to him, still with an innocent smile and immediately quickened her pace.

Disgruntled with failing to frighten the young girl, Fatinelli quietly turned and walked back out.

When he was sure to be out of range of earshot, Maria leaned in close to Zita and whispered:

"You have to get used to the Signor quickly, my girl. He is very demanding."

"If it is God's will, my work will be done as requested," replied Zita with a look on her face as though she had been spoken to with praise.

The food was all ready in time for the dinner and the family's guests couldn't complain with what they had been offered. Zita was kept on call until the last guests had left, clearing away and washing the plates without showing any sign of fatigue.

It was early in the morning when she was finally allowed to go to sleep. She knelt down at her bedside and despite having worked constantly throughout the day, spent over an hour saying her prayers.

She was already up and about in her attic space at the break of dawn, which considering it was approaching June meant that she had slept for little more than four hours. She continued with her task of cleaning away the dust while retaining deep concentration in prayer. She had sat in silence as she focused her mind on her sacrifice to God until it was time to begin her first duties of the day.

The dining room was not quite clean so Zita took a bowl of water and a cloth and set about scrubbing the floor. She didn't notice when Signora Fatinelli came in and stood in the doorway watching Zita with anger in her eyes.

"Girl!" she shouted at the top of her voice. "How dare you not stand up when I enter the room!"

Zita quickly looked up, put down her cloth and stood up

looking at the wall in front of her.

The Signora noticed that the young girl had not appeared to be slightly unnerved at her sudden screaming.

"You have a lot to learn if you expect to remain in this house."

"Please forgive me, madam. I am still learning the correct ways to address my superiors in different situations."

Signora Fatinelli almost felt put in her place by such a well-considered response and was at a loss to speak further in a demeaning manner: "Good, make sure you learn it as soon as possible."

"Indeed, your grace."

"Carry on with the cleaning, then."

The Signora walked out of the room then quietly sneaked back to check if Zita was reacting to her words but all she saw was the girl continuing to scrub the floor in the same manner as when she had previously entered.

Zita calmly continued with her work, moving between the dining room and the garden where she had to fetch more water from the well. Filipe was collecting all the different types of leaves that he could find. As no-one from the family or among the staff knew anything about trees or what they were all called, he decided he was going to give them his own names once he was sure he had found all the different kinds.

He turned around and noticed Zita waiting at the well for the bucket to fill. She appeared to be murmuring to herself as she looked vacantly above the trees. When her bucket was full, she took it back inside. Filipe was bemused with seeing her behave like this and it reminded him of some of the poor people that he had seen in the market who spoke to themselves, although they were often much more agitated than Zita was.

He continued inspecting his leaves and had kept them safe in his cap. He wanted to know how many he had found so took them over to the wall and laid them in a line on the ground next to it so that they wouldn't get blown away by the wind.

Just as he had finished laying them out, Zita emerged from the house once again. She walked in front of him and smiled as she went to the well. Filipe didn't say a word but just watched her to see if she would act in the way he had seen her before.

He kept completely still as she pumped the water. He couldn't see her face very well from where he was so he leaned forward to see if her lips were moving, which they were.

When she had finished, she walked back to the house and Filipe, with the manner of a young boy for whom social etiquette was not fully developed, wanted to find out why she was behaving like this.

"Zita," he called politely.

"Good day, Master," she replied with a smile.

"Are you well?"

"I am very well, thank you for asking."

"Were you singing just then?"

"Singing? No, I was speaking."

"Speaking to yourself?"

"No!" she laughed. "I speak to God."

"What do you mean?" replied Filipe. "You need to go to church to do that. Or pray by your bed."

"God is always here. I always want to be active in his presence. I talk to him about all the things that happen around me."

"Mmm, I see. Well, I was just wondering."

"That's no problem. I see you are doing well with finding your leaves."

"How did you know I was collecting leaves?"

"I like to pay attention to everything here. I have seen you when I have been going to the well. Your collection is growing well."

"Do you know the names of these trees?"

"Unfortunately not. I hope I will know more about them as I grow up. Do you know their names?"

"No. I am going to give them my own names."

"What a lovely idea. Please tell me when you have decided. It is a beautiful act to perform."

"Yes, I will."

"I have to get back to work now. Sorry that I have to leave you so soon."

Filipe watched her motionlessly as she delicately glided back through the doors.

Zita finished cleaning the dining-room and Maria beckoned her into the kitchen to have something to eat.

"You've been working hard all morning, Zita, come and eat."

"Thank you, Maria, but I am fine. There is plenty of work to do."

"Don't be silly. You will collapse if you keep working this hard without a break."

"Hard work is my penance, Maria."

"Your penance? What have you done wrong, my girl?"

"My mother died when I was young and God has His reason for taking her away from me. It is my duty to prove myself to Him."

"Well, that may be so but we are mere mortals and we need to stop to be replenished from time to time."

Yes, you're right but I must be quick so I can get to cleaning the other rooms."

"Take a seat, young girl, your feet must be aching."

Zita sat down even though she didn't feel any tiredness in her feet. She knew that Maria was her superior so she should obey her as it would be rude to God if she didn't do what she was instructed to do. She ate a piece of bread with two small tomatoes and didn't say a word unless she was spoken to.

"You seem to have settled into this job very well, Zita. How are you finding it?"

"Oh, it is wonderful. I feel so grateful for being accepted here."

"Don't you feel that the Fatinellis are being too hard with you?"

"No, not at all. It is God's will and I am happy to accept that."

"But you are such a young girl. We've had other servants here that have lost their jobs because they have broken down under the stress."

"Then those other servants have not known how fortunate they were to be given a job in such a beautiful place."

"You are very positive, but let me know if you have any difficulties. I have seen a lot in the twenty or so years I have been here."

"Thank you. You are very kind but I don't believe I will have any difficulties."

Zita went back to work and she diligently completed her tasks by nightfall, ate a little more and retired to her room to spend her free time kneeling by her bed, telling all she had to say to Her Almighty One.

3. In the morning, Zita rose three hours before she had to start work. She had been given permission to go to the church each morning before starting her chores. She listened attentively to the mass before returning solemnly to her place of employment.

Upon her return, Signor Fatinelli saw her as she went through to the kitchen.

"Where have you been?" he shouted at her from behind with his usual intention of startling her.

"Good morning, sir," she smiled as she turned around and bowed to her master. "I have been to mass and it is such a pleasant morning."

"You have to start work soon, you know."

"Yes, sir. I was going to start early as I made it back here with plenty of time left."

"Oh, I bet you think you are so clever for getting back early."

Zita looked at him for a moment, not really understanding what he mean by this.

"Don't stand there staring at me, you horrible child!" he bellowed into her face. "Make sure you never arrive here late."

"No, sir. I will always be here early to start my duties."

Fatinelli crossed his arms as he tried to instil his domineering attitude into this girl who was tiny compared to him. He looked venomously into her eyes, expecting her to cry.

Zita waited patiently to be given permission to leave his presence and go to the kitchen. Her face showed no signs of either fear or happiness. She appeared like a cat from which it was quite impossible to tell her feelings.

After a few moments, Fatinelli realised his plan had not worked and he yelled at her to go away. Zita bowed her head and walked on her way as though she had not been interrupted in any way.

The ruthless master of the house stormed into his office and thumped his fist down onto his table in anger. Even though he knew he had failed, his upbringing and his work didn't allow him to feel that and he cursed the gentle girl as though she had betrayed him in an unforgivable way.

His wife, who had heard all the commotion, along with everyone else in the house, entered the room. She was used to his outbursts and was just as guilty of them herself so didn't appear to have even suspected anything was wrong. She had come to ask him if he had everything he needed for his trip to Florence that he had to take that morning.

"That girl thinks she's so smart!" he sneered at her. "She looks at me with those big, sad eyes like she is ignoring whatever I say!"

"I'm sure she just doesn't understand. She is still very young, remember."

"Don't you defend her, woman!"

"I'm not. I just mean that we'll have plenty of opportunities to show her her place. I bet you she cries herself to sleep every night!"

"I hope so. She deserves it. Stupid little peasant that she is. She ought to think herself lucky that we have let her come and work for us."

"Don't worry about that now. You have important work to do this week. Do you have everything you need?"

"Yes, is the horseman here yet?"

"You have breakfast to eat first." she replied and left the room, knowing it was fruitless continuing the conversation while he was in this mood.

Signor Fatinelli continued fuming after his wife left the room. He was half-hoping Zita would cross his path as he went out so he could lash out at her once more, but also half-hoped he wouldn't see her in case she took his words in her stride again. He wasn't going to be defeated by a small child.

Zita had gone into the kitchen to help Maria to prepare the breakfast. Maria watched her to see if she was upset but Zita just went about finding the knife to gut the fish that the Fatinellis would be served.

"Good morning, Zita. Are you all right?"

"Good morning, Maria!" she said with a smile as though she had just woken up from a beautiful dream. "I am very well. Mass this morning was delightful."

"I mean with how the Signor just treated you."

"Well, I didn't really understand what he meant but it's all finished now. I have to get on with preparing the fish."

Zita sat down a the table and tried her best to remove the insides and the bones. Whilst living with her mother, she had not had any opportunities to eat fish and certainly not prepare them so it required a lot of concentration to get it right. Maria had told her what she needed to do and once the instructions were clear to Zita, she would engage in the process like it was a life or death operation.

Maria watched her and could see how engrossed she was. She was doing it well, if a little slowly but that would come with time. Overall, her efforts were worthy of great praise and she left her to finish it while she prepared the rest of the breakfast.

"Do you think this is good?" asked Zita after some minutes.

Maria leant over to inspect the fish. She carefully looked inside so as not to disturb Zita's handiwork.

"It is very good, I can't see any bones in there."

"I hope to God that I didn't miss any. I would be worthy of losing my job here if our master or mistress found any bones in it."

"They probably would throw you out but the fish seems to have been cleared well. Let me put it on the plate with the vegetables."

"Would you like me to take it through to the dining-room?" asked Zita without any fear of what the Fatinellis might say to her.

"I think it's best if I take it. I don't want you suffering unnecessarily. Signor Fatinelli is leaving this morning so you'd best try to avoid him for this short time."

"I'll clean up in here then."

Maria took the food through to the dining-room and went to find Signora Fatinelli to let her know it was ready.

The couple sat down to eat and the Signor looked reproachfully at the food.

"Did that girl prepare any of this food?"

"She helped me to slice the vegetables, sir." answered Maria, willing to take the blame if any bones were found in the fish.

"Hmm," he mumbled, unable to think of any criticism that could be attached to performing such a task.

"Zita is a very hard-working girl, sir. She doesn't cut any corners and she focuses very hard on everything she does."

"Thank you, Maria. That will be all." interrupted the Signora, pre-empting a tirade that she might have invoked. She gestured for Maria to leave the room.

The Fatinellis enjoyed an untainted breakfast without finding any pieces that may have been disagreeable. The master of the house soon left to spend the rest of the week conducting business in Florence, leaving his house in a moderately calm state.

This episode didn't leave Zita feeling relieved. It never entered her head that there should be something to concern her. She continued her hard work in exactly the same manner as she always did and she was as untroubled as when Signor Fatinelli was present.

4.   Zita continued working for the family throughout her childhood years. She kept to the same routines and tolerated the same and even worse punishments and abuses from the Fatinellis. However, as she moved more towards adulthood and Signor Fatinelli became older and weaker, he eventually gave up trying to break her down. She seemed to be untouchable. Maria stood by her side whenever Zita needed protecting but it was clear that she hardly needed it as she would happily move through her days unflustered even if she had been physically beaten.

She had been worked deliberately hard at times, often sent on errands to deliver messages to acquaintances many hours away. Sometimes it mean that she had to walk alone through heavy rain for hours with no shelter. Yet she always returned with a smile on her face as if she had merely been to the end of the road and back. Even when she was half-drowned, the solution was simply to dry herself off and change her clothes.

Some of her fellow servants couldn't understand how she could tolerate so much and they put it down to her being simple. They poked fun at her but found it about as useful as poking fun at a docile animal with no concept of language. Instead, the other servants would just make jokes about her to themselves as they knew they could not make her react to their bullying.

It was normal for the servants to complain about their masters behind their backs. This is the human way. It is another thing to actually confront the aspects which one doesn't agree with. That requires strength whereas the former is nothing more than a weakness. Zita knew that it was fruitless, not just to complain in secret, but it was not worth wasting one's own time, energy and patience on behaving in a way that would bring no reward. Besides, in her mind, God would know everything that she, and everyone else, thought at all times and to even think malicious or mildly negative thoughts would be viewed badly by God. Zita based her own actions and thoughts on two principles: either something would please God or it would displease Him.

She viewed her fellow servants with sympathy when she saw they were troubled by their masters' demands and abuses. It would affect them greatly in most instances and she wished they could tolerate it like she did. For them to become angry or bitter was not going to help their cause but for her to simply accept that something unpleasant had happened and was then finished with was more useful for her own spirit if she took it as nothing worth worrying about.

Zita had ample time to develop her tolerance and ability to overcome such issues immediately. She would practically be a victim of some sort of mistreatment every day or every other day but as long as she thought that God would view her as His loving child, she believed that she was doing things the right way.

Whatever the circumstances, Zita would be willing to undertake any work that she was ordered to do. Other servants may have been reluctant if the work was likely to exhaust them or if they felt it was unnecessary but Zita viewed work as a punishment of sin and as a remedy for the spiritual disorders of their souls. By working hard, every person would develop their souls and make more smoothly their paths towards heaven. She saw being idle as sinful and believed that God would not treat idle people so favourably when the day came that it was their time to chosen to enter heaven or not. Her work was its own reward. Even though she would spend almost every day working for most of it, as long as she had the sanctity of going to church in the mornings and had a bed to sleep in, there was nothing else that she needed. She never asked for a day off and was rarely given one.

As she moved into adulthood, her unwavering desire to serve her masters had the invisible power of bringing her respect from them. They had never heard of a case where she had said a cross word against them. Nor had they ever seen her look miserable or reluctant to perform any task. But Zita had shown horror when she heard a colleague say a bad word. The very idea that someone could speak in such a way filled her with pity and she would plead with her masters that the guilty party should be removed from the household. She took on such episodes as though it was herself that had committed a terrible sin and to absolve herself and her co-worker, she would fast on nothing more than a small piece of bread and a cup of water, and she would sleep on the bare boards of the attic floor. In one instance she lived like this for a whole year.

In 1238, Zita turned 26 years old. She had been a devoted servant for fourteen years and had worked alongside Maria for the same amount of time. Other servants came and went depending on their ability to restrain themselves from outbursts against the family, their laziness to do their work or their lack of desire to remain in their positions. Maria was getting much older. In this year she was approaching 57 years of age and even though she had remained a strong woman whose character had been strengthened by working and living alongside Zita, she became subject to palpitations and was finding it difficult to continue with her work in the same manner that she had done for the previous thirty-four years. From the influence of Zita, she felt guilty if she had to stop what she was doing and have a sit down to catch her breath or wait until her heartbeat became regular again.

One morning, Zita had been making the beds upstairs and went down to the kitchen to help Maria with preparing the lunch. She opened the door but Maria wasn't to be seen. She must have gone to another room, thought Zita but as she walked around the table which was in the middle of the kitchen, she saw Maria lying on the floor.

"Maria!" she shouted. "Maria, are you all right?"

Maria was breathing with difficulty and her eyes were trying to pick out Zita as she moved towards her. She could only just make out a whisper:

"I can't move..."

"Oh, Our Lord, help us! Are you in pain?"

"My chest... hurts..."

Zita didn't know what to do. She called for someone in the house to come in and help her. The oldest son, Giuseppe, was the first to arrive.

"What's happened?" he asked before he, too, saw Maria on the floor.

"I don't know. She collapsed and her chest hurts."

"Is she breathing?"

"Yes, she's alive but I don't know what to do."

"Her chest? That must be her heart. Let me see if I can feel it beating."

"He put his hand onto her chest and could only make out a very shallow heartbeat.

"Can you hear me, Maria?" he asked.

She looked in the direction of his face but was unable to focus. She opened her mouth and although she could move her lips slightly, she couldn't speak.

"Do you know what to do, Giuseppe?"

"No, I don't think she's going to survive."

By this time, Filipe and Signora Fatinelli had come in along with three of the other servants. They gathered round to find out what was happening but no-one seemed to know what to do.

"This happened to my mother." remarked David, one of the servants.

They all looked round to him, expecting him to tell them what needed to be done.

"It's her heart, people said. She died the same day."

They all looked at him in horror before turning back to Maria, whose face was vacant. She wasn't responding to their questions and her lips weren't moving any more. After a short time, her breathing stopped and she passed away.

"Dear Lord, have mercy on her." called out Zita. "I'm sure you know she was a wonderful woman who never did anyone wrong. Please take her soul and let her rest with you in heaven."

The servants were asked to carry Maria to her bedroom. They fetched a blanket to lift her and placed her on her bed. The next day she was buried in the cemetery of St. Frigidian's church and her funeral was attended by more than fifty people who knew her and the Fatinelli family.

5.   The death of Maria was a huge blow to the whole Fatinelli household. After so many years of service, the home did not seem the same without her. Even Zita, who could overcome any burden or hardship was noticeably affected by this sad loss. She stayed longer than usual in the church and was allowed to spend time in the graveyard mourning and praying for her salvation.

When she returned to the house, she continued her work with a solemn air and everyone else left her in silence, knowing that she would be the one most affected by Maria's death as they had worked very closely ever since Zita first came to work here.

She was engaged in speaking to the Lord throughout the day, asking for his strength and support both here in the house and with Maria in heaven.

The following morning, Zita appeared to be as normal, conversing with people in her typical way and not relating anything to their collective loss. Those who she spoke to felt a little unsure how to react. Should they mention Maria to her or also act like nothing had happened? They guessed it was part of her mourning period and reacted to her as best as they could, not to upset her.

After a few days, Zita was called to the sitting room where the Fatinellis and the three children were waiting.

"Zita, it has been a very difficult time for all of us, especially for you, I'm sure." Signor Fatinelli spoke in the most peaceful way Zita had ever heard him. "Maria was a great housekeeper and we all agree that she did a wonderful job."

Zita watched his eyes as he spoke and paid no attention to anyone else in the room.

"The difficulty that we have to face now is that we have no-one to work as the housekeeper. As you know Maria took care of our finances as well as the general running of the household."

Zita continued to remain silent and motionless, her hands held together in her lap.

"We have discussed together, all of us in this room, and we would like to ask you if you would become our new housekeeper."

She looked at the other faces who offered her signs of respect and trust. She looked back at Signor Fatinelli who was staring at her intently from under his heavy brow which after so many years of looking in this way was now the only way he would look when he wasn't speaking.

"Sir, I very much respect your offer." answered Zita after a few moments. "I have learnt a lot from Maria over the years and she has taught me how she manages the finances."

She stopped and noticed that all eyes were fixed on her from all sides.

"It is God's will for me to serve you and I would be grateful to take on your offer and become your next housekeeper. I hope that, eventually, I will be able to do as good a job as Maria, God bless her."

The five members of the family all raised a smile simultaneously and moved from absolute stillness into one of joy, thrilled that Zita had accepted.

"I am... we are all very pleased to hear that, Zita." Fatinelli said as his brow lifted to reveal his unusually happy eyes. "My wife and I will instruct you as to what the role requires and we will help you with any questions you may have."

"Thank you sir, madam. I will do my best to serve your family to the best of my abilities."

"I'm sure you will," added the Signora. "We have complete faith in you. You have shown yourself to be strong and hard-working and we know that we can trust you with this responsibility."

"We will make a start on things in the morning, but first, you need time to get used to the idea of your new position." said the master.

On the way out, Filipe invited Zita to sit with him in the

garden as it was a sunny day and still warm at the end of September.

"I have always admired you, Zita." he said as they sat on the wall looking at to the garden. "I have always felt a good connection with you, ever since we were children."

"Thank you, sir." she replied. "I have always admired your desire to learn more and more."

"Yes, unfortunately, my father has not often been of the same mind." he stated with a look of displeasure. "He has only had it in his mind that I will continue his work along with Giuseppe. It really doesn't interest me."

"But sir, trading is a most noble of occupations. It is how this family has been able to look after itself so well."

"Yes, that's true. Look, I don't like it when you call me sir. It sounds too formal. Please call me Filipe. I see you as someone who is my equal."

Zita smiled at Filipe. "Are you sure? You will always be my superior."

"No, I won't. You and I understand each other. We like the same things. Please, call me by my name."

"If you wish, sir. Um, excuse me! If you wish, Filipe." They both giggled as they looked at each other, Zita looking very embarrassed and shy.

"If you need any help with your new role, don't think twice about asking me." he affirmed.

"Thank you... Filipe. I'm sure I will need some help, being your family's housekeeper is a very big responsibility."

"I don't think you will need much help at all. I have never known you to do anything badly or to not finish doing anything."

"Well, as you know, God has entrusted me with providing the greatest service to you all. I have always felt honoured to be here and do everything that is required."

"Of that, I have no doubt. You deserve this position. You have been my favourite servant ever since I can remember."

"Oh, sir. You are making me blush."

Filipe smirked as he looked into Zita's eyes. "I'm not 'sir', don't forget!"

6. The following morning, Zita met with the Fatinellis to discuss her new responsibilities. She was already well aware of what the job entailed after working alongside Maria for so long but now she would be expected to supervise and manage all of the day-to-day duties and delegate work to the other servants.

Signor Fatinelli explained how she would be expected to manage the finances. This included deciding how the money would be spent for general things such as food, but also to oversee payments made for other expenditures like business travel.

"I will, of course, be aware of how much money I have, more or less," explained Fatinelli "and I'm sure you wouldn't do anything you shouldn't do with my money, that's why I am trusting you with this responsibility, but I have to make it clear that I will be taking regular looks at the books."

"I understand, sir. I give you my word that everything will be accounted for. God is our witness at all times, and as you know..."

"... you would only do something if it pleases God, "he interrupted. "That's why I trust you, Zita. I just needed to make it clear, like I would to anybody."

"Of course, sir. I did not take offence at that."

They went through more of the details of Zita's new job and her first task was to organise the weekend's dinner where some new trading partners were going to be meeting Fatinelli to talk about expanding his trade in Pistoia. There were going to be eight visitors on the Saturday and the food and cleaning needed to be taken care of.

"Yes, sir. I can take Ana with me to the market to buy the food."

"You are allowed to send who you want now, Zita. You don't have to go any more."

"Oh, no! I like going to the market, sir. I couldn't miss saying hello to my friends there."

"Well, as long as all the work is done that needs to be done. You'll have to work out for yourself how to allocate people to different jobs."

"Not a problem, sir. I will do things in the same way that Maria did, God bless her soul. And don't expect me to give the dirty work to everyone else. I am still a servant like the rest of them."

Signor Fatinelli nodded to her and left the room. He wasn't too pleased that she wasn't going to follow his example and take a firm stance. He sort of knew that she wasn't likely to be like that but all his life he had been in a powerful position, ordering people about, whether they needed to be or not. It would always seem strange to him if someone didn't use their position to their own advantage.

Zita happily got on with speaking to the staff and saying what needed to be organised. Instead of simply telling them who would do what, she *asked* who would like to do what. This was not how things had ever been done before. Maria, although being friendly and reasonable, would simply inform them all of what she expected them to do. Tomas and David exchanged crafty glances at each other while the allocation of duties was taking place.

"We'll go and get the food," said Tomas. "We would like to do that for once." Tomas was the one who had first met Zita here and had always viewed her as 'that stupid child'.

"I don't think so," said Ana, sternly. "You'll eat half of it before it even gets here."

"Don't be ridiculous. You'd know it wasn't all here, wouldn't you?" David laughed.

"They can't be trusted with money," Ana added. "I'm sure they'd buy the cheapest things and keep the change."

"No, we wouldn't!" said Tomas. "That wouldn't be worth our while. We'd never get away with it."

"Ana and I are going to buy the food," said Zita. "That job I have decided for myself. The garden and the stables need tidying. Can you two do that, please?"

"Oh, again? We're always having to do that." sighed David.

"But you know how to do it and you do it well."

"All right... Come on, Tomas, back to the stables..."

"I'll get you something nice from the market if you do a good job." smiled Zita.

"What? Some old rotten carrots?" mumbled Tomas.

"Don't be silly, a nice piece of pork."

"Mmm, that sounds more like it."

"But you can only have it if you clean everything properly."

"Yes, my lady!" bowed the two men in jest and they went off to the garden.

"Do you think she'll really give us some pork?" asked David.

"I doubt it! Fatinelli would never let his money be spent on us."

"Yes, true. Come on, let's get to work but don't do any more than we normally do."

"What do you think I am, stupid?"

David stopped and thought about that for a second. "Yes, that would be the right word!" he laughed as he slapped Tomas on the back.

The two of them got to work in the fashion that they usually adopted, which was to do the job before dark but without straining themselves. They moaned about the family and wondered how they would be able to trick Zita if she was going to let them choose which jobs to do. They knew they'd have to be crafty and act like they wanted to do something that seemed difficult but they always had ways of making light work of things. They were not treated well by the family because of their attitude and were paid the minimum it took to keep them there.

They made a start with clearing the hay in the stable but were intrigued as to how work was going to be with Zita as the housekeeper.

"Do you think she'll be able to do the job?" Tomas asked.

"Probably. She's not as stupid as you've always made her out to be, you know," David answered.

"What do you mean 'me'? You did it just as much as I did. I don't know, it's going to be strange having her ask what we want to do. We're going to have to think of new strategies now to make sure we get the easiest work."

"Well, that doesn't matter. I'm sure we'll have her wrapped round our fingers soon enough."

There wasn't too much tidying that needed doing so, in their usual fashion, they spent most of their time lying in the hay, talking about anything and nothing. It was at one of these times when before they knew it, Zita was standing in the doorway, looking at them.

"Have you finished your work yet?" she asked.

They both jumped up like startled mice and surprised themselves as to how nervous they were to be faced with their new superior.

"Oh, sorry Zita." David stammered. "We were just having a short break. We've been lifting so much hay that our backs are hurting."

Zita looked at them without expression and they couldn't work out if they were in trouble or not.

"There's still the other stable to do, as well. Can you please try to get that finished today, too?" she asked calmly.

"Yes, of course," Tomas replied. "We'll have it finished before it gets dark."

"Thank you," she added and walked out without another word.

Tomas and David looked at each other. Both of their hearts were beating fast and they realised that each other felt like small boys who had been caught stealing honey from the jar.

"I don't have a good feeling about this," Tomas said.

"There's something strange about Zita. I can't figure out if she's angry or not," David thought out loud.

"That's it. It's hard to tell from her face if we're going to be punished or not. It's like she's our mother or something."

They got back to work and went to the other stable. This time, they didn't speak very much and got the job done more quickly than they ever had before. They went back into the house, still expecting to be told off.

In the kitchen, Zita thanked them for finishing so quickly. She explained that she hadn't been able to get any pork but as they finished long before it was dark, she told them she would try her best to get them something good to eat the next time she went to the market.

From that day, the two rogues' attitude to their work changed considerably. They couldn't tell what it was, if it was respect for Zita or fear. Now, if she asked them if they could do a certain job, they would accept it without asking if there were any alternatives. They responded to her quiet authority and none of the other servants experienced any trouble from them. After a couple of months of working under the command of Zita, they both began to take an interest in going to church. Influenced by her devotion and her permanently calm manner, it was as though they had been encouraged to follow her example without her ever asking them to consider it.

7. Over the following weeks, the feeling of the whole household changed. Zita not only conducted herself in her usual peaceful and forgiving manner but as she became established in her new role, she was viewed more as the centrepiece of the whole family. When she walked through a room or a hallway the calm that she took with her seemed to flow all around the room. Other servants who may have been working when she entered could feel this serenity before even seeing that she was there. Signor Fatinelli had not been so influenced by her manner as he was still working away from home a lot of the time or deep in thought about it when he was at home. His way of being was to take no notice of the feelings of others but only to concern himself with issues that directly affected himself. He treated Zita with much more respect now, of course, but his stubborn ways were unlikely to be altered at this time in his life.

She continued to pay little attention to him when she knew he was in a bad mood. If she needed to speak to him at these times, however, she would ask him if they could make an appointment to speak whenever it suited him better.

It was dinner time at the Fatinelli house. All of the family were sat around the dining table waiting to be served. Zita had managed to maintain the same rituals of preparing the meals as before and, if anything, the presentation and quality of the food had improved. She had shared her dedication of being meticulous with ensuring that every piece of meat and fish was prepared to the highest standard and, although Signor Fatinelli expected his meals to be as good as those he ate in the finest restaurants when he was travelling, he noticed how delicious they tended to be these days.

Ana had brought in their starters of tuna with a fresh salad and the family wasted no time with getting into their meal.

"So what are your thoughts about how Zita has settled into her new role?" the father inquired of the family.

"It's fine," said Giuseppe. "Everyone's getting on with their work well enough but it all seems very quiet around here how."

"That's obviously down to Zita's influence," added Filipe. "She's got them all working in her own special way."

"Special? It's a bit dull if you ask me," Giuseppe said with an air of displeasure. "You hardly hear them talking now. It's like they are all still in mourning."

"No, it's not that," said Filipe. "It's more of everyone being calm and dedicated to their jobs. I don't think they're unhappy."

"I agree with Giuseppe," said Beatrice. "I know they should keep quiet around us but it seems as if they are all marching towards their graves. I don't think that attitude is going to look well when we are entertaining a party of important guests. Can't you talk to them, father? To try to get them to look a bit happier?"

"Servants are supposed to not be noticed," he answered. "They work here to serve us and our guests and otherwise, they shouldn't be noticed."

"Yes, I know that," she added. "But whenever I see them around the house, it makes me feel miserable, too."

"I'm surprised you even notice them at all," said Filipe. "Just carry on treating them as if they are not there, or like they are just ants scurrying around doing what they have to do."

Beatrice knew that he was being derogatory with that statement.

"What do you expect me to do? Of course I notice them, they work and live here. I just don't want to have my good mood brought down because of the unhappiness that they bring into the room with them."

"They're not feeling unhappy, anyway," he responded. "They are just doing their work without any fuss. I admit that it's a lot quieter in here now but I feel it as though it is calm and peaceful."

"One thing that does annoy me," Beatrice continued "is that awful dress that Zita still wears. She's had that for years and she never wears anything else."

"So give her some of your dresses then. I'm sure you've got plenty that you don't wear any more."

"Those are not work clothes. She needs something more practical but she looks like she should be begging on the streets with what she wears."

"You know she doesn't have any interest in new clothes," answered the father. "I've spoken to her about that before but there's no getting around her."

"You should just buy her a new dress and make her wear it," she said. "Then she wouldn't have any choice. She's our servant. She has to do what she is told."

"It's not as easy as that. You know how she is. She always has a way of explaining why God would not approve of her wearing something new. It would be an insult to tell her she is wrong."

"Well, when we have guests here and they see her in that, they would have a good reason to be unimpressed with the state of our house."

Signor Fatinelli thought she had a good point with that comment. Whereas it wasn't important for guests to see servants dressed up in expensive clothes, to have them looking dirty was another thing, especially when they were serving food. He decided he would have words with her and try to get her to see this point.

"I think the most important thing is that Zita is doing a marvellous job," said Filipe in her defence. "She has got the other servants working a lot harder and I haven't heard of any complaints from any of them for a long time."

"Why do you jump to her defence so much, Filipe?" asked his sister. "Have you got feelings for her or something? Just remember who she is. She's just a servant like the rest of them. She comes from a poor family. In fact, she doesn't even have a family. She's here to serve us because that's all she's good for."

"I have a lot more respect for her than I do for you," he added with contempt. "She works practically every moment she is awake and what do you do? You just go around acting as thought you are the queen of the world."

"How dare you! You come from the same family as me. I don't see you going around in rags. Perhaps you should and you two can go somewhere far away and get married!"

"All right, you two," bellowed the father. "When we eat in this house, nobody speaks like that!"

The siblings were well-conditioned enough to know not to respond to their father when he used that tone of voice. Beatrice looked across the table scornfully at her brother but he just looked down at his plate and continued eating. It was true that he had a lot of respect for Zita and he also cared a great deal for her well-being.

The weather had turned colder and wetter. Zita had left the servants undertaking their chores around the house while she went down to the market. Despite the drop in temperature, she still wore nothing more than her old dress, which she had now used for at least eight years. Now that she wasn't growing any taller, she didn't have the need to own any other garments. But she barely noticed the cold. After years of being sent on tasks while walking through the driving rain, she was hardened to the weather and its changes. But she knew that most other people were unable to cope so well.

Zita knew practically everybody in Montsegradi, but not just because it was a small village. She made it her duty to know the people as well as she could because she believed it was her responsibility to take care of anyone who was in difficulty; whether it was due to their health or their poverty. And Montsegradi had its fair share of people who suffered in various ways.

On the road to the market, there were beggars who needed any scrap of food they could get. For some years, Zita had, with the agreement of the Fatinellis, been taking any pieces of food that were left over from family meals. Even if it was only bones with barely visible strips of meat still on them or the ends of vegetables that would otherwise go into the rubbish, Zita collected whatever she could to help the poor and infirm of the village.

She received thanks from those people who still had their mental faculties to remember who she was, although she didn't think that their gratitude was even necessary. There were others who were delirious and never understood a word she had said. They didn't know who she was or what she wanted with them but unknown to them, she helped them a great deal. She would lift them out of puddles and cover their thin and fragile limbs with the shreds of clothes that hung off them. Zita felt profoundly that if these people couldn't have any more clothes than this, then she certainly didn't deserve any more. There was no justice in that in her mind; she would be cheating them if she came out to help them while wearing new or a variety of outfits each time.

Zita had tried to talk with the women who worked in the market to ask them to give any scraps of food that they couldn't sell to the unfortunates on the roadsides. But as they were also living in poverty, they needed to eat whatever they could as well. There didn't seem to be any other way of helping the people apart from sharing out the meagre amounts of food that were already here.

"Good morning, Zita!" called Teresa, who sold her vegetables. "You look frozen."

"Good morning, Teresa. I'm absolutely fine, like always."

"I don't know how you do it. I'm here wrapped up in my blanket and I can still feel the wind."

"Yes, but you have to stay here all day. When you're moving around like me, you don't feel the cold so much."

"I still can't believe your master doesn't buy you a coat."

"I have no need for one. This dress is all I need."

"As you wish. So what can I do for you today?"

Zita bought her usual vegetables. She had been given a little extra money in case there was some good meat to buy but there was little available that day. She wanted to give some food to give to a poor, fragile old woman who was lying nearby. She appeared to be at the point of death and Zita could only just make out that her chest was moving with her feeble breaths. She felt she needed to act immediately if she was going to save her, so she left her bag with Teresa and paid for a small cup of milk and an orange. She went over to the old woman, whose name nobody seemed to know, and gently lifted her head off the ground. The woman barely stirred but she was still alive. Zita rested her head in her arm and raised the cup to her lips. Despite not being aware of what was being done to her, she retained the instinct to drink the milk in tiny sips. Around them, people passed by and glanced over at this event. Most of the passers-by paid little attention as they were beyond the point of caring for anybody except their own families but one or two, whom Zita had helped in some way in the past, gave her a smile or a wave in acknowledgement of her generosity.

She peeled the orange and carefully fed small pieces to the woman. Again, instinctively she was able to recognise it as food and let it into her mouth. She had very few teeth left and those that she had were loose and brown but she managed to swallow the small pieces of segments that she was fed.

She managed to eat three segments when she opened her eyes for the first time. She soon found Zita's face and gave her a faint smile. Zita said a prayer for her and wished that she could have done more for her but this was the situation that always found herself in. She could help someone to survive another day and she would remember who needed the most help so that she could check on them the next day that she came to the market and give them priority.

Once she felt she had done all she could for the time being, she collected her purchases and went on her way back home.

She hadn't even left the market area when she recoiled in horror at what she'd just done. She almost broke down when she realised what had taken place.

"Oh, Lord, please forgive me," she called out loud. The people around her looked in astonishment as she fell to her knees as though she'd had a heart seizure. She dropped her bag of food and clasped her hands together with her face desperately turned to the heavens. The village-folk stopped what they were doing and gathered round her. They wondered what had happened to the woman who takes care of anyone who needs it. They hushed each other so they could hear her pitiful cries to the heavens.

"Lord, my saviour, I have sinned." The people looked at her then at each other thinking that she had lost her mind. "I have taken my master's authority into my own hands. I wasn't supposed to spend his money on something that wasn't for the family. I didn't ask for his permission. Oh, please forgive me. I will confess to my master and the whole family immediately."

She crossed herself and stood back up. She picked up her bag and saw the mud on her legs. The onlookers continued to watch the spectacle that they still didn't understand clearly. Zita felt very ashamed. She was unaware of the group gathered around her but tried desperately to wipe the dirt off her skin and her dress but couldn't remove it. Nobody offered to help her as they didn't know what she might do if they approached her. She left them in a state of complete confusion and rushed back to the house, almost in tears.

When she reached the house, she went around the back to enter into the kitchen. Before she could confess, she needed to wash herself the best she could. She couldn't possibly speak to her employers looking like she did. She managed to clean her skin and remove enough dirt off her dress so that it didn't look too noticeable. Ana came into the kitchen while she was doing this and saw her forlorn face.

"Whatever is the matter, Zita?" she asked with her eyes open wide.

"Oh, Ana. It is terrible. I spent some of the Signor's money on food and drink for an old woman who was nearly dying."

Ana listened but didn't know what to say next. Had she heard her correctly? It appeared that Zita was so terribly upset because she had done something good. She continued to watch Zita as she wrung the water out of the bottom of her dress into a small bucket.

"I must go and confess to them," she said. "I pray that they will forgive me."

She walked past Ana, who was also confused. She turned her head as Zita left via the door into the hallway.

The Signor was checking his accounts in his office when he heard a faint knock on the door. He didn't like being disturbed when he was making sure that his figures added up correctly. He continued working on the list of numbers and after a few seconds, the knock came again.

"What is it?" he shouted, disgusted by the impertinence of someone interrupting him in such a persistent manner.

Zita slowly pushed the door and, as timid as a lamb, could barely be seen through the opening. He squinted to make out who was playing games with him, ready to give them a verbal, if not physical, punishment for this behaviour.

"Please, sir," Zita managed. He craned his neck as he couldn't tell from the voice who it was. "I must speak to you. I have something to confess."

He scraped his chair back and stood up. He was the latest person to become bemused with this unusual sight of Zita acting so ashamed. His anger had completely gone as he told her to come in and close the door behind her. She did so and stood by the door, afraid to come nearer.

"Whatever is the matter, my girl?" he inquired with the voice of a loving grandfather to his tiny granddaughter whose woeful eyes could change anyone's mood in an instant.

"Signor," she bowed her head. "I spent some of your coins on a cup of milk and an orange for a poor old lady who was lying on the ground."

He, too, could not think of anything to say at this point and waited for her to make herself clear.

"I acted spontaneously and didn't realise I had done it. Of course, now I realise it was without your permission."

"My permission? But you are well-known for helping people out. You don't need my permission or anybody else's for that."

"I mean I spent your money on something else that you didn't give me the authority to do so. Sir, I am truly sorry and ashamed at having sinned. I have spoken to God to ask for his forgive...."

"Zita," he interrupted. "You haven't sinned. Of course you may spend a little money to help someone in need like that. I'm sure an orange and some milk is not going to upset my accounts to any extent."

"But I should have asked you first, master..."

"How could you? I wasn't there. If it helps, I give you my authority in retrospect. As always, you did something that the Good Lord would admire and bless you for."

"Oh, master. Really? You are so kind. I will never do that again. I promise you."

"Zita, calm down. You have done nothing wrong. Let it go. Have a sit down and drink something. You must relax. There is nothing that I need to forgive you for."

He walked over to her and took her arm. He opened the door and led her into the kitchen. She sat down on a stool and he beckoned Ana over to make her some tea with leaves he had procured recently from one of his trade journeys. He whispered to Ana to take care of her. He had no experience of looking after someone who felt so timid and he knew he was out of his league to stay there with her. He tapped Zita on the shoulder and went back to his room.

"Zita, I don't understand what has happened. Can you tell me?" Ana said.

"The Signor said he has forgiven me... no, he hasn't forgiven me. He didn't need to... He said everything is all right, but I still feel terrible."

"Terrible about what?"

She tried to explain and eventually Ana thought that she understood what had happened and why Zita felt so guilty. She brought her the tea, which was an unusually kind act from their master, who ordinarily would never let the servants drink some of his tea. This was only for the upper classes to drink in his house.

Meanwhile, he sat in his office with his elbows on the desk and his chin resting on his clasped hands. He wasn't so perplexed with Zita's apology and call for forgiveness as he was for acting in a way that was so unlike him.

8. The family ate at their normal time that evening and Zita resumed her service to them. The father had not mentioned anything about the day's episode to them and he watched her carefully out of the corner of his eye when she entered the dining room and looked at her fully when she turned to walk back out. The other members of the family did not notice their father at this time. They had already learned that he saw it as being rude if they looked at him without being engaged in conversation with him. Even Signora Fatinelli knew when to keep her eyes down, despite the fact that she could be just as ruthless as her husband. There had been plenty of times when she had put him in his place, but this happened when her instincts of anger took the place of her considered actions. If she was in control of herself, she would be more wary and tread more carefully with him. The rages that he had displayed throughout his life would make any grown man cower and he had certainly done such a thing on many occasions.

But he had been thinking about how he had acted with Zita. She seemed to have been able to stop one of his rages dead in its tracks. He hadn't actually realised that nobody had been able to achieve such a feat before; that was just how he was and he never gave it any thought. But the fact that Zita, his poor, unassuming head servant, who would never attempt to step out of place and speak to her superiors in a way that didn't fit her position in life, affected him simply by appearing at the door in the fashion that she did made him contemplate his own character.

When their main course had been placed on the table and the servants had left, the table was as quiet as it often was. The rest of the family could feel that there was something on their father's mind and they wouldn't risk asking him what it was. He, in turn, couldn't bear to reveal to them how he had been silenced by a woman so much younger than him who hadn't even attempted to reproach him.

Beatrice wanted to ask him if he had had words with Zita about the discussion regarding her dress but felt it better if she remained quiet at this time. He, too, thought about bringing up the subject of Zita but he didn't how to speak of it. He knew he had been moved by her delicateness but to admit this to his family would make him look like a small child. He decided that he would need to think about it some more before speaking to anyone about it; that is, unless he chose to keep it known only to himself.

That night, Zita went to her attic space as she always did. Before the family, she appeared to be back to normal and working in her typically calm manner. She knew it was her responsibility to appear this way while she was working or in the presence of any other person but during the evening she had her mind focused on something else. From many years of practice, she had learned how to subconsciously be in communication with God even if she was attending to something else or speaking to someone else. She always felt that connection and had raised it to a more concentrated level while she was working. She had been fully aware that she should be making more of an effort to mend her ways. Even though the Signor had said she didn't need forgiving, her way of thinking told her that she still owed the family a great deal for spending a tiny amount of their vast wealth on something that had not been authorised.

She knelt down at the side of her bed and stayed in direct communication with God deep into the night. Not for one moment did her concentration falter. Nor did she feel any discomfort from remaining on her knees for several hours. They were pressed against the rough wooden floor but Zita was a strong woman; much stronger than she gave herself credit for. To be able to do something like this was not an act of strength in her mind, it was simply what was required of her. More than being a servant to the family, she was a servant to God and if he willed something to happen, that was how it must be. She acknowledged that he had given her the test when faced with taking care of the old woman and she felt very guilty for having failed at it. She meditated on how she should be more prepared for such events and how to deliberate over the options at her disposal before deciding on how she should act.

When she woke early the next morning, she felt ready to start a new chapter in her her life. She believed that she was a stronger person and would now always be in control of any situation that she was confronted with.

After she returned from church, she entered the kitchen to instruct the staff as to the jobs needed for the day.

They were sat around waiting in a casual manner to be asked what they would like to do but today, they weren't asked, they were told. Zita had already decided who would be better suited to which job and she explained to them that from now, they would receive their orders in this way. She spoke in her calm voice and didn't give the impression that she was being authoritative with them.

This came as a surprise to them all but, like the Signor, they were so taken over by seeing Zita act differently, they didn't know what to say. They collected themselves and set off to do their respective jobs.

Signor Fatinelli was not due to go on his next trip for another two days. He would be travelling back to Pistoia to finalise his deals with traders so that he would be in control of the merchandise they would be selling on their stalls. He didn't have all the details in place yet but had been so sidetracked with thinking about Zita, that his plans were falling behind schedule, which was a rarity for him.

It was not that he had been touched by her generosity for helping the old woman. She was already well-known for performing such acts. He was touched by her meekness upon entering his room and by her showing him that he could put someone's feeling before his. As he was now in his fifties, he had gone through several decades of putting himself before anyone else who might have impeded his way at all. He went to locate Zita, who was cleaning his wife's parlour with the kind of diligence of someone who had been given the ultimatum of life or death depending on the quality of her work. He quietly entered the room and with the silence that lay between them, said in an almost nervous voice:

"Zita, when you have a moment, could you please come into my office?"

She stopped her work, stood up straight to face him and replied:

"Yes, master. I will be there straight away."

He nodded his head slightly and left the room. He returned to his office and went to sit behind his desk. Before he reached it, he stopped and thought that it would seem too official if they spoke in that way, so instead went over to his armchair that faced another similar chair with a small round table between them.

He sat down and for once, actually thought about how he should be sitting. Upright or more relaxed, leaning back? He wanted them both to feel comfortable while they were talking.

Before he had adjusted his body to a position that he was happy with, Zita knocked on the door.

"Co...." he had to stop to clear his throat. "Come in."

She entered the room and seemed like a different person to when she entered the previous day. Her posture indicated confidence and her face was one that seemed ready to receive any disagreement. She looked over to his desk and noticed him out of the corner of her eye as he beckoned her over with his arm.

"I prefer to sit here today. Please, come and sit down." He pointed to the armchair, which had always been a seat that was out of bounds for any servant.

Zita did not waver at this unusual proposal and she walked calmly over and sat in the chair. She rested her hands in her lap and sat upright, prepared to listen to whatever it was he wanted to say.

"And how are you today?" he asked, looking at her uneasily as though he was the one under interrogation.

"Very well, thank you, sir," she replied. As a servant, she was used to only directly answering the questions posed to her by her masters and not elaborating on them unless she was asked to. This was not something that happened as a rule.

"And... have you recovered from your upset yesterday?"

"Yes, thank you, sir. I have spoken with God and now I feel that I have been forgiven by Our Saviour."

"Very good. That's the main thing... that you feel calm again."

She nodded her head once to show that his words reflected the truth. She waited for him to reach the true nature of the conversation that he had requested her presence for and she noticed that he was seeming to be a bit stuck for words. She showed no expression of any kind but appeared like a statue to him, which made him feel even more uncomfortable.

"Right, well, I wanted to speak to you about something."

"Of course, my master."

"I have been speaking with the family about how things are going with you being the head-servant and so on. To see if they think things are working well..." Zita remained stationary as it was not yet her cue to speak. "They are happy with the new circumstances but we all think..." he didn't want to be seen as the sole person who had this opinion. "that it would be better if we bought you a new dress." He paused to see if she would react yet.

"I thank you sincerely, sir, for the offer but like I have said before, all I need is this simple dress that I can wear for work. I need nothing more."

"I understand but we were thinking that it would look better, when we are entertaining guests, if our staff looked more presentable. You see, and I don't mean to cause any offence, you have had that dress for I don't know how many years and it's looking beyond repair these days."

Zita could see his point but she was reluctant to have money spent on her.

"So, will you let me buy you something new to replace that dress?"

"Sir, I would prefer that the money be used for something more worthwhile."

"What do you mean?"

"I mean, and forgive me for mentioning this again, but when I wrongly spent your money yesterday, maybe the money could be used to help other people out in a similar way."

"Well, if I did that, I would always be spending all my money on hundreds of people that I don't know."

"With respect, sir, I am only talking about small amounts that could mean the difference between life and death for some people."

Signor Fatinelli was not in agreement with helping the poor. To him, the poor have always been a species of human far below himself and people who have no good reason to exist. He had never given a single coin or piece of bread to a beggar but somehow, he couldn't give a straight-out refusal to Zita for her idea.

"How about this," he said after mulling things over. "I will give you a few coins that you can use to feed someone if you let me buy you a new dress."

Zita considered this and thought that as long as she would be given some extra money, maybe the compromise was worth agreeing to.

"It's a possibility, sir," she said while clearly deep in thought about the suggestion. "But I will only have a dress that is the cheapest one that can be found. Maybe then, if it is to your liking, the leftover money that you had been intending to spend on the dress can be used to feed the poor people of the village."

Fatinelli breathed in deeply through his nostrils. He was used to people bargaining with him when he was working but to have a servant following the same procedure was something that left him feeling just a little uncomfortable. He looked at her for a few seconds. He wasn't aware that he was staring at her with eyes that said 'You are out of your depth' but Zita, still sitting up straight, looked at the painting of the wall behind her master. This gave her an air of confidence and strength, and the appearance that she wasn't about to back down on her words.

"All right. I will do that. I will buy you a new dress when I go into Pistoia, just something simple but also something that my guests would like to see. Then I will give you the extra money when I return and you will be at liberty to use it as you wish."

Zita's facial expression finally changed as she gave a grateful smile.

"Thank you, sir. The Lord will look upon on you most favourably for such a kind act. Will there be anything else, sir?"

"No, that's all. Thank you, Zita. You may go back to your work."

She got up and confidently, but more lightly, strode out of the office and went back to cleaning her mistress's room. Her mood had lifted considerably as she cleaned every part of every object in there. Fatinelli, however, was not in a similar mood back in his room. He remained seated on the armchair but slumped back into it as he thought: I've just had a servant make a deal with me on her terms. How can this be so? In all my business arrangements, I've always made sure that I will benefit the most from them. And now, I'm giving my money away to the poor? Is this what happens to men like me as they age? She has a very clever way of getting her way. So quiet but difficult to argue against.

He thought about whether he should try to behave in such a way when conducting his business. As soon as he thought it, he knew that he could never act in such a manner. Everyone would think he had finally lost his mind.

9.   Despite the fact that Zita had talked her master round to agree to what she would prefer to see happen, she wasn't at all proud of her efforts. As she continued her work throughout the rest of the day, she spoke to the other servants but didn't mention the talk once. She carried on as though nothing out of the ordinary had happened. It was a similar situation for Fatinelli but it wasn't something he was proud of. He preferred to keep it quiet so that no-one in his own family would hear of it. He wondered if, through Zita, the word would get out and he contemplated meeting with her again to ask her not to mention it. But another strange feeling came over him – he felt ashamed to ask her about this. During the afternoon, he would spontaneously make the move to go and find her but something stopped him. He felt like he was having to beg for her forgiveness and that she would look down on him like his mother did when he was a small child. He even remembered the days when he was in this position. His mother was the last person in his life to be able to command him to do anything. She died when he was fifteen and his father had died when Fatinelli was only nine, and as he became parent-less he took control of his own life and the incorporated the sternness of his mother when conducting all affairs of his life. But now he felt like he was once again a young boy who was having to speak to his mother in the hope that she wouldn't beat him for coming in with dirty clothes.

The family had dinner at their usual time and Zita served them as she always did. The Signor monitored her with scrutiny again but not to make sure she kept in line; to wonder if she acted any differently with him. As she came in and went out of the dining room, she appeared to be her usual, meek self; not drawing any attention to herself but simply performing her duties in the way that she was supposed to. It all seemed to be as he had hoped.

When the family were left to start eating, there was also the possibility that one of his kin had heard something about the incident. Fatinelli remained quiet throughout dinner in case anyone asked him about Zita. The others conversed only with small talk and it appeared that no-one was any the wiser about their brute of a father showing that he actually did have the potential to place someone else's feelings before his.

After she had finished her duties, Zita went to her attic space and knelt by the bed to say her prayers as she always did. She gave special thanks to God for allowing her to work for such a kind master and asked Him to bless the Signor for allowing her a few coins to use to buy food for the poor souls who lay in the streets. She promised that she would wear the new dress but make nothing of it; for her it was only a necessity in which to do her work and to keep herself warm enough.

Fatinelli was in his bed at the same time, mulling the day's events over in his mind still. Such a tiny thing had disturbed him greatly. He wondered if he had done the right thing or the wrong thing by submitting to Zita's request. Even though he believed in God and went to church and prayed, he still considered himself to be his own master but it felt like the carpet had been pulled from underneath him and everyone else was laughing at him. The only consolation he got was that it seemed that no-one else knew.

The next day was when he would be travelling to Pistoia. As soon as he awoke, he remembered what had happened yesterday. He tried to block it from his mind and think about what he needed to do when he got there. He travelled shortly after breakfast and arrived in time for lunch. He went to his regular restaurant and met his associates. They discussed their plans to expand their control of goods being imported into the region. It was a matter of establishing that they would pay out a greater sum of money to buy more goods that would give them more profit in return as well as wheedling out some of their smaller competitors. They would be meeting with others involved in the trade business that afternoon and staying overnight until everything was agreed and signed.

After talking for a couple of hours, Fatinelli asked for a few minutes to walk around the market by himself. He said that he wanted to assess the situation and get a feel for who could be taken control of more easily. His colleagues granted him permission, of course, and he left.

The real reason he wanted time to himself, as you may guess, was to find a new dress for Zita. He entered the market where most of the traders knew him well. He was liked by some but feared and despised by many more for his ruthless and unfair tactics. He wondered if it would appear strange for him to be searching for a dress that was obviously not for his wife. He put on his usual stern persona and strutted around while the traders bowed their heads as he walked past their stalls. He went to one that sold simple dresses but felt conspicuous about looking at them. He pretended that he was simply looking around him at what was going on and trying to glimpse at the garments out of the corner of his eye. He didn't want it to be known by anyone what he was here for so he beckoned over the stall-holder to speak with him.

The woman, a strong-minded and experienced dealer in her forties came over to him.

"What can I do for you, sir?" she asked with no hint of being imposed upon.

"I need to buy a simple dress."

"For your wife, sir? I don't think I have the kind of dresses she would wear!"

"No, it's for my head-servant."

"Oh, really?" She looked at him confused. "Is she ill, sir?"

"No, she's fine. Why do you ask?"

"Well, sir, I would have thought she should go to buy her own dresses. What an honour it is for her to have her master to give up his time for her!" She laughed out loud. Fatinelli was shocked to hear her speak so directly and condescendingly to him. He quickly looked around him to see if anyone had heard what she just said. There were a couple of peasant women who were grinning to each other but trying to hide their faces from him. He turned back and looked sternly at the woman.

"Look here!" he said firmly under his breath. "Don't you ever dare speak to me like that again. I can have your stall closed down."

She looked at him with a wry smile on her face. She hadn't been affected by these words.

"What colour would you like, sir?" she asked without blinking.

"I don't know. Something simple. Just one colour, maybe a dark blue."

"Of course, sir. I have just the thing." She went back behind her table and picked out a dress that was dark blue and would reach down to the ankles.

"Something like this, sir?"

He looked at it to gauge whether it would be the right size for Zita. He wasn't sure but it looked long enough.

"How tall is your lovely servant, sir?"

"I don't know, she's about the same as you."

She placed it against her body and it reached her toes.

"Is she slimmer than me?" she asked. She was a fairly plump and noticeably bigger than Zita.

"Yes, she's very thin. Would that fit her?"

"This is for thinner women, yes. I'm sure she could adjust it if she needed to. After all, she is a servant. I'm sure she's an expert at sewing."

Fatinelli was getting itchy feet from having to be trapped in this ordeal. He asked how much it cost and the woman tried her luck by raising the price that she would normally sell it for. He accepted it straight away so that he could make a quick exit. He didn't care if he had had to pay three times the price he was given. Whatever it cost, he knew he would have to give Zita some extra coins, anyway.

During the rest of the afternoon, his perceived humiliation at the stall put him in a bad mood. He had lots of meetings with traders and associates but came across as being even more grumpy than ever. Everyone else treated him very carefully and feared for their lives but this meant that Fatinelli was able to secure the deals very much in his favour and he would be making even more money than previously. He could have taken his carriage home and got there before midnight but chose to stay away and have some time to himself. He didn't want to drink to his and his friends' success and they knew it was not worth their time to try to convince him otherwise. He went to his guest house, tried to read in the lounge but found it hard to concentrate, so went early to bed.

The mixture of his success from his business deals, his humiliation from the market-woman and his submission to his head-servant didn't mix well for him and he tossed and turned for hours, only getting about four hours sleep before the sun rose and it was time for breakfast.

10. Fatinelli returned home the next day. After speaking briefly with his wife about the success of his trip he called for Zita to meet him in his office. She duly obeyed and again, as though it had now become the norm for them, they sat on the armchairs. She asked how his trip had been and he informed her of the success that he had and how his wealth was likely to increase even more. She congratulated him on his achievement then waited for him to speak.

He reached down to the side of his chair and lifted up the dress.

"This is what I found for you. I hope it is to your liking." He passed it over to her.

"Thank you very much, sir. This is a very nice garment." She unfolded it to get a better look at it.

"Is it simple enough for you?" he asked.

"Yes, thank you, sir. I hope you didn't spend too much on it."

"It's not important how much it was. You needed a new dress and I am the one who must cover the costs."

She thanked him again. She didn't want to stand and see if it was her size as that would be too conceited of her, so she folded it again and would take a look at it when she finished work. She sat patiently to see if he had anything else to say or if he would permit her to get back to work.

"I'm sure you remember that we talked about giving you some money to help the people in the village." She was secretly pleased that he had brought the subject up. "How much money do you think you would need?"

"Sir, that is completely your decision, of course. It is your money and I will leave it to your judgement as to how much you would be willing to give."

He didn't really like this response. He would prefer it if she gave him a number. He had no idea how much would be useful to her. She helped a countless number of people but he also wasn't prepared to give her enough to feed them all.

"How about if I give you three silver coins?"

"Oh, sir. That is far too much, surely." Zita had been expecting to receive one silver coin at the most. That would only be enough to buy a few pieces of food and drink for a small number of people but she was used to helping with the minimum that she had.

"Too much? You take care of my accounts here, Zita. I think you are aware that I can afford to give you three coins."

"Sir, if you insist. That would be most generous. I'm sure the Lord would look down on you very approvingly if you could do that."

He reached into his money pouch and took out three silver coins. He handed them to Zita and told her to spend them as well as she saw fit and to help as many people as she could. She stood up and bowed to him in thanks.

After she had served dinner and finished cleaning for the day, she took the new dress and went up to her attic. She tried it on and it was a little too big around the waist and about three finger-widths too long at the hem. She said her prayers to God and again, made a special mention about her master and his generosity. She took her sewing equipment and worked into the night adjusting the dress so that it would be ready to wear the next day.

Anyone who knew what she was doing would have thought she was excited to get new clothes, especially something as beautiful as this rich, deep blue garment. However, Zita was unmoved by this; to her she had a duty to make it look like it fitted her properly so that she would look respectable to the family and their guests. And as her master had been out and bought it for her, it would be impolite if she appeared to him at breakfast time in her old dress.

She had finished it by two o'clock in the morning, said another prayer and went to sleep.

In the morning, she put on her new dress as soon as she had

washed herself. She went to church as always and received some interested looks from the other attendees. They complimented her on her new attire and said she looked beautiful, respectable, and more like a member of the nobility. Zita didn't approve of such comments and she merely gave them a polite thank you and avoided getting into conversation. She thought that those people were focusing their thoughts on something far too trivial and hoped they would be able to return to the purpose of their visits. She said a prayer for them and asked God to forgive them for their momentary loss of principles.

She returned to the house to start preparing breakfast and had similar comments from her co-workers.

"What a beautiful dress, Zita!" remarked Ana.

"Thank you," she replied without any sign of pride or conceit.

"It fits you really well. Where did you find that?"

"Signor Fatinelli bought it for me and I adjusted it last night."

"The Signor bought it? You mean he went out to get it?"

"Yes, but please, Ana, it is nothing important at all. He believed that I needed a replacement dress so that their guests would not be offended by my appearance."

"But it looks so nice! I'm not used to seeing you look so pretty!"

"Ana, I do not approve of such comments. Forgive me for saying but I am not here to look pretty. That is of no consequence to me. It never enters my head to be concerned with how I look, as long as I look presentable for my position as head-servant. I intend now to wear this dress for as long as it holds together and to do my work to the best of my ability, as long as God will allow me. I appreciate your compliments but I would prefer it if you didn't speak to me about such matters any more."

"I am sorry, Zita. I just thought..."

"Don't be sorry. Just please act as though nothing has changed. Let us continue to prepare the breakfast."

They got on with their work and served the breakfast to the family. Of course, they all noticed it but being of a higher social class than her, merely gave her brief compliments as to how she looked professional and that it was a nice colour.

Signor Fatinelli was able to pass the purchase off very quickly, saying indifferently that he just picked it up because he saw it by chance in Pistoia as he was on his way to meet someone. The new dress and how it made Zita look caught the attention of Filipe more than the other family members. He silently observed Zita as she entered and left the room and his eyes returned to his plate as soon as she was out of sight. He made no comment as it was not the done thing to talk about the servants unless there was an absolute need.

It was a pleasant day and the first one in about a week when it wasn't raining in the morning. Filipe wanted to take a walk in the garden as it had been too wet for him to do so recently. As he was inspecting the bushes and trees as he often did with such devotion, Zita came out to the well to collect some water. He watched her from behind as she filled the bucket. He touched his lips with the leaf that he had just picked and walked over to her.

"Good morning, Zita," he said, giving her a little surprise as she didn't see him approaching.

"Oh, sir! Um, Filipe... you made me jump!"

"I do apologise. I just wanted to see the dress that my father bought for you."

"Oh, yes. It was very kind of him and I needed a new work dress." She had filled the bucket and stooped to pick it up.

"Please, let me," he offered. This was a rare event but he had carried the water for her before if he was in the garden at the same time as she was.

"Thank you, that is most kind."

"Not at all. I wouldn't want you to get your new dress wet on its first day at work!"

She smiled and thanked him. He held the bucket but didn't

start walking. He was looking at her with a hint of a smile on his lips. He had always had feelings for Zita, even though she was a servant. She liked him but never forgot that he was still her superior, regardless of how clear he had made it that he was friendlier with her and treated her more like an equal.

Zita felt uncomfortable and was too shy to look him in the eyes. She couldn't bare it any longer even though they had stood there silently for only about five seconds.

"Shall we go inside?" she asked.

"Of course," he answered. He knew she was very shy and let the moment go by remarking how lovely a morning it was and how the plants needed the light.

Zita got back to work with cleaning the surfaces in the kitchen as Filipe went back into the garden and over to the trees. He pretended he was inspecting them as before but really he was looking through the gaps between the leaves at this beautiful young maid in her lovely new dress.

11. Zita desperately wanted to go into the village so that she could spend the three silver coins given to her by her master. She had to wait until the next day as there was already enough food in the house to suffice for the day's meals. She almost always had the self-control not to be overawed about anything but throughout the day, she found herself drifting off to think about what she could buy and who needed her help the most. When she noticed herself doing this, she realised she had sometimes paused while she was working to make her plans. She made her apologies to God and got back to work and completed every job with the utmost diligence.

The next morning, she became even more anxious to get to the work that, even though she considered everything that she did to be important for its own reasons, filled her with even more passion to carry it out. This meant that she could possibly save people's lives and help them recover from their illnesses that had been brought on by the wind and the rain, as well as the uncleanliness of living in the streets.

She once again had to keep herself calm and remember that she needed to make sure she bought the food for the household and performed her duties correctly without being lost in the time that she wanted to devote to those who she cared most deeply about.

She thought that the wisest way of going about this would be to take Ana with her, who was then taking the family's food back and start preparing it and getting on with other jobs while Zita was out. Tomas and David were given more than enough work to keep them busy in her absence. While they were finishing the cleaning after breakfast, the two men pondered what was happening with Zita these days.

"I reckon she thinks more of herself since she got that new dress," Tomas grumbled quietly to David as they were walking out of the kitchen.

"That's about three days' work that she's given us. Does she expect us to do it all today?"

"I don't know but I hope not. She's acting more like the Fatinellis themselves with those orders."

"She didn't even tell us why she's going to be away, today," David noticed. "She doesn't usually keep secrets from us."

"Well, maybe she's preparing a secret party for us," Tomas replied sarcastically. David laughed and they went off to start cleaning the stables yet again.

Zita and Ana got themselves in order and set off for the market. She hadn't told anyone about the coins and what she intended to do with them. In her mind, it was a necessary task to fulfil and nothing that needed to be discussed with anyone, any more than cleaning the bedrooms would be.

Ana was curious though, and as they were now together with no-one else around, she thought she would ask Zita what she was going to do.

"I have been given a little extra money by our generous master and after we buy our groceries, I shall be using it to buy food for the needy people that I take care of."

"Oh, that's interesting. But do you need so much time for that?"

"I don't know how long I will need. The more time I can give, the more I can help them," she explained. "That is why I was so specific with the jobs that needed doing for today. If I am gone for a few hours, the work at the house should be taken care of adequately in my absence."

Ana understood but it still sounded a little mysterious to her. She was used to this, however. Zita was not one to give all the details about her thoughts and plans. She knew that she would be doing a good thing, no matter what it was.

They arrived at the market and Zita wasted no time with selecting the food that they needed. Ana took the bags and Zita asked her to hurry back as Ana was having to do the work of the two of them while she was away. Ana didn't say a word, although she thought it was quite a direct order.

She returned to the house and David came into the kitchen while she was putting the food away.

"Hello, Ana," he said. "Did you find out what Zita is up to?"

"Yes, I did," she replied, also not wanting to go into details. She was not a friend of David as she didn't like his mannerisms and always kept their conversations to a minimum. "It's a good thing that she is doing, like always."

"Is that all you're going to tell me?" he asked sternly. He often treated Ana as though she was his own servant.

"David, we have a lot of work to do with Zita being away. Let's just get on with it."

David looked at her with fire in his eyes but she ignored him and carried on with getting ready to start cleaning. He shook his head and went back outside.

"So, what did you find out?" asked Tomas when he had returned.

"Nothing. She wouldn't tell me anything other than she's doing a good thing," he said, mocking Ana's voice.

"Well, that doesn't make anything clearer. Zita's always doing her good things," Tomas said without conviction. "A proper little angel she is. Especially when she leaves us to do her work for her while she spends the morning with her friends."

While they moaned about their work and their head-servant, Zita was already fully engrossed in what she was doing. She managed to convince some of the stall-holders to give her slight discounts for buying more food than usual. She got as much fruit and milk as she could. She wished she could buy meat but without being able to cook it there, it was no use.

"What are you doing with all that?" asked Marco, one of the sellers. "Another banquet, is it?"

"Absolutely not. This is for the poor people here," she told him. "My master has been most generous, Lord bless his soul."

Marco didn't know what she was referring to and nodded his

head in silence as she put more things into her bags which were bulging almost to the point of splitting.

She knew exactly who she was going to find and in which order as the various problems that they had was stored in her head as though she was a highly-trained doctor who knew his patients inside-out. She first went to the old lady that she had quite possibly saved from dying a few days earlier.

She tenderly raised her on her arm as before and helped her to eat small pieces of fruit that she cut off with a small knife that she had brought from the kitchen. At this time, she thought about how she was going to divide up the food that she had bought so that it would have the maximum benefit for the people who she was going to tend to.

Fortunately, it wasn't raining that day and it was mildly warm but she still made sure that the lady was wrapped up in her threadbare clothes.

She next saw to a man who had scabs and sores on both his legs and feet. He, too, was in a delirious state and couldn't take care of himself. Zita gave him some milk but as he had only three or four teeth left, she had to soften the fruit with her fingers so that he could eat it without having to chew it.

As she went to visit six other people with similar predicaments, she thought that the food and drink alone was not enough to save them. As long as they didn't have sufficient clothing and nowhere to stay, they were always going to be ravaged with illnesses. Despite doing more than she ever had done before, she felt like she was still failing them.

She stayed around the market area for more than two hours, all the time being watched by the villagers who, even though they were used to seeing her act so selflessly, were intrigued by her staying there for so long.

Most of the villagers were supportive of her, but there were still some who were so miserable with their own lives and lived in poverty and on the brink of starvation themselves, who gave Zita comments that reflected their desperation and frustration:

"You should just leave him to die. He doesn't even know where he is."

"Your wasting your time. She's never going to get better."

"He's eating more than I will today but I don't see you giving me anything."

Zita was used to hearing such comments and she understood their reasons for saying such things. However, she could only sympathise with them at that moment and was not affected by their harsh words.

After she had shared out all the food and drinks that she had bought, she knew there was nothing else that she could do that day so headed home. To any outsider, she would have been seen as a great saviour but Zita was deep in thought all the way back. She wasn't satisfied and was thinking about what else she could do.

12. She spoke very little to anyone else at the house. She took up the tasks for the day alongside them and the others could tell that there was something on her mind. However, they could see that she was not looking emotional so they left her to herself and they carried on with their work. This continued for a few days; Zita had been thinking about whether she should ask her master for another donation but decided it would be above her station to do so. It was not part of her authority to meddle in her master's affairs and suggest that he conduct himself in any other way than he chose to. All she could do was hope that he would offer to furnish her with more money before too long so that she could help in more ways than just feeding the poor.

Fatinelli had been organising his new strategies for expanding his business over the next days when he received a message. He was loathe to discover there were some complications. It took less than a minute before everyone in the house also found out that there was something to his disliking. He bellowed out a string of expletives that almost shook the walls. The Signora detected that this was something really serious. It was commonplace to hear him shout but something of this magnitude spelled grave problems. She rushed into his office to find out what was the matter.

"My plans have been thwarted!" he shouted at her. "It appears that there are other merchants who have arrived in the region who have a great deal of influence."

"And what are they doing?"

"There's a danger that they are going to encroach on my business connections and get control of some of my trade."

"Who are they? Where are they from?"

"I don't know for sure. They have come from the north, possibly Genova and are looking to expand their trade here. Apparently, it is a group of people who have considerable wealth and the power to usurp me."

"Oh, no," cried the Signora. She always supported her

husband's business plans as, of course, her extravagant lifestyle depended on the amount of income they made. She had already been planning what to spend their increased profits on.

The two of them moaned and cursed and thumped their fists against all manner of furniture in the office when they heard a knock at the door. Zita calmly opened the door and her serene glow was one that could not be admonished in any way. The Fatinellis stopped instantly as she presented herself to them. She, along with anyone else in earshot, had heard all the news for herself. The moment that she came into the room, she raised her right hand which seemed to send out a strong message for them to calm down.

"Sir, if you don't mind me saying, I'm sure you have nothing to worry about. You will just have to adjust your plans and try to reach a compromise with these new traders."

The Fatinellis looked at her in astonishment. This was one of their servants, a generation younger than they were who simply glided into the office and put an abrupt end to their hot-headedness. Zita went on to explain that not everything can work out exactly as one would wish and sometimes, concessions had to be made. Even if he couldn't get all the share of the trade that he wanted, he could still get control of a little more of it.

"And if you will excuse me, sir and madam, I must leave and get back to my work." With that, she bowed her head and left the room.

The Fatinellis were lost for words. At first, they stood staring at the door as though a ghost had just come in and put a spell on them and then quickly flitted away. They almost didn't want to look at each other, they felt so humbled. After a few moments, the Signor finally said, without looking at his wife:

"Perhaps she's right. I suppose I will have to look at things differently."

"Yes," she replied, still in a state of disbelief. "I'm sure there is an answer."

Without any further words, the Signora, whilst looking at

nothing in particular, rather she was mesmerised by what she had just experienced, walked out of the room and went to her own parlour.

Signor Fatinelli stood there and his brow wrinkled into its usual state as his eyebrows lurched down his forehead, and wondered what on earth was happening to him these days. This was most unsettling; his head-servant was not only able to convince him to do as she wished, but she could stop him in his tracks when nobody would normally dare to be in his presence when he was in that state of mind.

He sat down in his armchair and tried to make sense of these bizarre events. He thought about what Zita had said and as he weighed up his options, realised that she was indeed right. What else could he do? Try to have the merchants removed by force? Things like that always have their repercussions. She had given a very sensible suggestion but at that moment, he was unable to start thinking about how he was going to change his plans. He needed time to remember who he was and how he did things. Except, it felt like he was now someone else.

Filipe had been upstairs and heard all the commotion. He couldn't understand why it had suddenly stopped but didn't know if he should go to find out. Had his father suffered a heart attack set off by his anger? There was no sound. Surely his mother would have screamed out if that had happened. He thought he'd better check.

As he was walking down the stairs, he saw Zita in the hallway, dusting the ornaments on the table.

"Zita, what happened to my father?"

"Nothing," she answered, not realising what his concerns were. "He is fine."

"But... I just heard him shouting... my mother as well... and then it just stopped."

"I just gave him some advice," she answered as though she had performed the most obvious of duties. "He ought to adjust his plans accordingly."

Filipe raised his eyebrows and looked at her while he tried to work out what this meant. She had given him some business advice? And he listened? That didn't make any sense to him.

"And he didn't collapse or anything?"

"No, he's quite calm now. Hopefully, he's just relaxing in his office."

He nodded pensively and quietly walked over to his father's office. He needed to find out for himself what state he was in. He was more than used to these outbursts but if he was caught in the middle of them, he knew how to get away without becoming involved in them.

He knocked the door, opened it and put his head around it; with the door covering the rest of his body, there wouldn't be much of a target, should his father launch a tirade at him.

He saw his father sitting in his chair.

"Is everything well, father?" he asked as calmly as possible.

Fatinelli didn't hear the words as he was still deep in thought. A couple of seconds after his son had spoken, he realised there was someone there and he turned his head to him.

"What?"

He repeated the question.

"Yes, yes..." he answered as though he still didn't know what he had been asked. He said no more so Filipe thought it best to leave it at that. He went back into the hallway and closed the door.

Something strange is going on, he thought. I think he must have gone into shock about something. Zita noticed him standing there, looking blankly at the door and asked him if he was all right.

This time, Filipe was the one to not hear the words and he looked across to her.

"Sorry?" he said.

She repeated the question.

"Well... yes, I think so. Did something strange happen to my father?"

"Unless my calming him down was strange, nothing else to my knowledge," she informed him.

He looked at her and this feeling of confusion and silence was becoming contagious. He walked back down the hallway towards Zita and went back up the stairs to his bedroom. As he turned the corner on the stairwell, Zita looked up at him; he was still somewhat disconnected. She smiled to herself and moved down the hallway to clear the dust off the mirror.

13. As she was still hoping that her master would give her some extra money, Zita decided to make some use of the old dress that she now no longer wore. It was old and had become thin but she thought she could at least use it to make some items that her needy neighbours could benefit from. After work, she thought about what would work the best. If she tried to make something big like trousers, she would be limited as to how much could be made. The people that she helped rarely had anything on their feet so she concluded that it would be a good idea to make foot cloths. This way, even if they only lasted for a few days or weeks, at least they could get some relief from the cold and the dirt that surely contributed to their illnesses. She used her own feet to work out the size and shape that would work best.

The first ones she made were quite rudimentary. The shapes, when she tried them on herself, meant the cloths were not too tight. She knew that it wasn't important how they looked but if they were going to stay on their feet and keep them warm, she needed to do better. The next pair she made were an improvement on her first effort and she continued way into the night. Because of her devotion to her position and duties, anything else that Zita wanted to do had to be done in her own time; and that only came about shortly before midnight and until the point where she couldn't keep awake any longer. It never crossed her mind to ask for time off work to do anything else that appealed to her. She had been given permission to spend time helping after she received the three silver coins but unless her superiors gave her permission again, it was not her place to ask.

She managed to make eight pairs of foot cloths and because of the shapes she had cut out, she ended up with a fairly large amount of fabric that she would try to weave into a hat at a later date. She was tired by this time so begged the Lord to have mercy on her for not continuing her work any more at this hour.

She had produced some things that would be useful so prayed that she would be viewed favourably by God.

After breakfast the next morning, it was time to go to the market again. Zita collected her foot cloths together and went to get her bag. As she was walking to the kitchen, Filipe met her along the way. He noticed the bundle of fabric in her hands and asked her what she had. She explained to him what she had made and he was impressed with her ingenuity. Before he could say anything more, she carried on her way as she was on a mission and didn't want to lose any time.

Zita went as quickly as she could to the market and similarly, she quickly went from stall to stall to find all the food she needed. The stall-holders watched her rush by and she appeared to be in one of 'her states', which meant that it was probably best not to ask as they would probably be left understanding very little of the situation from her brief answers. She was watched avidly by all as there must have been something behind her frantic movements.

Zita then proceeded to locate her patients. She was sad to know that she couldn't give them any food or drink on this day but completed her set task of placing the foot cloths on the feet of those who needed them the most. As she had made each of them without any measurements, the sizes varied so she tried and changed them accordingly, and on more than one occasion went back to someone whom she had given cloths to already and swapped them for smaller ones so the last person she saw had a pair that were bigger and fitted better.

As she dashed between people who were aware of her being with them briefly but not knowing who she was, her appearances and disappearances left one or two of them a little agitated. Zita felt she needed to move as quickly as possible so that she wouldn't be questioned as to why she had been gone so long.

It had not been told to her explicitly but even if she had

returned home later than usual, the family trusted her greatly and would never think of questioning her. They knew her motives to be honourable and charitable and of course, she worked faultlessly around the home. However, Zita didn't assume such things and she only acted in ways that she thought would be appropriate to her work position.

As she finished donning the last foot cloths, she stood in the road and, out of breath, looked back on her task. It looked like she had done it the best that she could have, so she quickly said a prayer for the Lord to take care of them and hurried back to the house.

Filipe was there again as she returned. He was doing this quite deliberately as he wanted to take an interest in her activities more. He, too, was often left unclear as to what she sometimes did or said so when she arrived, he followed her into the kitchen and questioned her to find out the details.

She gave him a simple explanation but he asked her give more details. He was more persistent than usual because he wanted to understand her better. She darted back and forth in front of him as she put the various foods in their places. If he had been her master, she would have stopped to explain as he much as was requested but she knew Filipe was much more casual so sometimes treated him as though he was another of the servants.

He asked to her clarify herself every time he had not understood her clearly and he finally reached the conclusion. She was wanting to get on with her work promptly so asked him if there was anything else. He saw that she was desperate to go so smiled and shook his head. As Zita zipped out of the kitchen, he sat there pondering what he had found out. He was glad to have a more complete story of this event and as he stood up to leave the room, he thought to himself: She is a *good* woman...

He went through to the front room and stood in front of the window. He didn't have any pressing business to attend to that day and just wanted to think about things. He watched the birds as they flew between the trees in the front garden and thought about what it takes to be a special person. His father was seen to be important, of course, mainly because of how wealthy he was but also because of the influence he had in his work. But was he special? He thought that if he asked people who knew him that question, they would probably not use that word to describe him. He knew very well that his father was seen as a fearsome man. Many people thought that due to some of his decisions and actions they were left at a disadvantage and there was no question that he had more enemies than friends.

Was Filipe perceived in the same way as his father? He hoped not; he was not into ruthless trading but because he worked alongside his father and people knew about their family connection, there were bound to be people who automatically didn't like him. But he knew that he made a effort to be friendly with people. He spoke to them politely and smiled at them. He always tried to be fair when conducting business, but mostly he just followed his father's plans and had to apologise at times for how things were. It was not his fault and he would explain that if it was his decision, he would have done things differently but that didn't win him much affection if the traders were going to earn less money.

He had no idea about what people in the market thought of Zita. They must all know her, he thought, but he was rarely in Montsegradi and she was rarely anywhere else outside the house these days. He had his own opinion of her firmly established but felt guilty of it at times. He had nothing but respect for her regarding the commitment she showed to her work. He also approved of the work that she did to help the poor people but, again, as he didn't move in the same circles that she did, he was oblivious to who they were and how they suffered.

He moved to the question of who should be considered more important: him or her? According to the beliefs of society, Zita was merely a peasant who was lucky enough to work for a wealthy family. Most people in the surrounding area didn't eat as well as the family's servants so the servants must be seen as lucky. He thought of Zita's sleeping quarters. He sighed as he wondered how she could go on sleeping in the same place since she first came to work here. He never went up there but as it was the attic, he assumed it must be horribly dusty and probably had birds nesting in there. He had never known anything like such a place; of course, he only stayed in the most expensive dwellings whenever he travelled and his room was always free of dust and meticulously taken care of.

But who did the most important work? Was it him just because he, together with his father and brother, made the money that was used partly to feed the servants? It could be thought of an important thing for their sakes. They might be servants but at least they lived there as well. It was surely much better than living in those tiny stone and wooden houses in the villages. Surely his family had some saving graces.

But look at what Zita did, he thought. She works practically every hour of every day, doesn't complain about anything and even uses her old dress to make foot cloths for the people who live in the streets.

He looked up at the clouds and felt a shiver run down his spine. Zita is a very special person, he concluded. I might be from a wealthy and noble family and she just a peasant girl but if things were different, I think I could see myself marrying her...

He heard the door handle turn and Zita walked into the room.

She didn't notice him as she got straight to work with her cloth, wiping the tables, picture frames and everything else. He now stood with his back to the window and just watched her as though he was invisible. He saw how she moved her arms, how lightly she stepped around the room and how gracefully she behaved. She doesn't look like a peasant, he thought. If she was dressed like my sister or my mother, no-one would think she had been born a peasant. She looks like she should be a member of nobility.

He had impression that music should be accompanying her movements. He had the desire to take her hand and dance with her. He almost couldn't stop himself from striding over to her and taking her into his arms. He flinched as though he was about to be overcome with instinct. But he found that he actually stopped himself by coughing and trying to regain his composure. Zita jumped and turned around to him in surprise.

"Filipe!" she said, with her hand to her mouth. "I'm sorry. I didn't know you were there!"

"That's all right," he said, feeling his cheeks turn red. He thought he had been caught in the middle of an inappropriate act. "I was just... looking out the window..." He smiled nervously to her. He didn't lie, he had really been doing that.

She noticed that he was looking nervous.

"Is anything the matter?" she asked.

"No," he retorted quickly and began looking even more flustered. "I'm... no... everything is fine."

Zita could see right through him but he being her superior, even though she knew he preferred to see them more as friends, knew it wouldn't be right to make any comment.

She acknowledged that everything was indeed fine and she carried on cleaning. He could feel his heart beating so hard, he thought it must be visible through his shirt. He wished it would calm down but then noticed that his cheeks were burning. He put his hand up to his face and felt very embarrassed. She was facing away from him now so he quickly made his exit and ran up the stairs to his bedroom.

He sat down on his bed and couldn't believe what he'd just been through. He must have looked like a small child who had been caught stealing from his father's purse. Could she guess what he had been thinking about? No, surely not, he was just standing there. But she must have known there was something on his mind. He didn't know what to do. He felt like he wanted to stay alone in his room and not see Zita or anyone else for the rest of the day. And I'm twenty-three years old, he thought. I feel like a five year old...

14. It hadn't occurred to Zita that Filipe had any feelings for her. To her, he was a member of the family that she worked for but he stood out because he was more approachable than all of the others. She didn't need to act so formally with him but she still maintained a certain distance between them. This was not because she expected anything to develop between them. That was out of the question but not just because of their vastly different statuses in society. Zita was here to serve God. Everything that she did needed to be willed by God. She was paying for the sins of others and it would be a great sin if she was to become involved with anybody, let alone someone of a different social status. Since she had joined the family, the only objective she had in the house was to perform her tasks correctly and diligently. She had no interest in becoming married to anyone, nor did she entertain the idea of it. That was not a part of her life.

She had no problem with that way of being. She had never thought of what it would be like to be a man's wife. She already effectively lived her life in that kind of role without having anyone to call her husband. She hadn't created a barrier between herself and any man in terms of a relationship, it simply wasn't a concept to her.

Thus, she continued her daily work without giving any thought to what had happened in the front room of the house. To her, nothing had happened but to Filipe, it was still an embarrassing episode. He wanted to apologise to her for at least appearing strange, even if he hadn't tried anything untoward. He had spent a couple of hours feeling uncomfortable with what had happened but by the late afternoon, he had calmed down sufficiently to show his face again.

He had thought intensely about how he was going to explain himself to Zita so that he wouldn't embarrass himself further but could finalise the issue as quickly as possible.

He found her in the kitchen and immediately began his

speech:

"Zita, I am sorry about earlier. I understand that I must have appeared to behave strangely with you but it was just that I was lost in thought and like yourself, hadn't noticed we were both in the same room. That is why I was lost for words, so again, I apologise."

She listened to him carefully and kept her face expressionless.

"You have nothing to apologise for. Things like this happen sometimes and it was exactly the same for both of us."

Filipe thanked her and couldn't think of anything else to say. If he had tried to start another conversation, he would probably get his words twisted even more so he told her that he wouldn't keep her from her work any longer and left the room.

As he walked along the hallway thinking about whether he had conducted himself well and ended his problem, and therefore his anxiety, Zita continued her work with absolutely no such thoughts in her head. She paid no more attention to what he said and didn't attempt to work out why he felt he needed to come and apologise to her.

The following Saturday, Zita was seeing to the household accounts. She was surprised to see that the total income for the Fatinellis had increased notably and that, as usual, there was a great deal of money left over for them to spend as they wished. As she had silenced her masters so effectively a few days earlier, she naturally felt like she was able to converse more freely with them. There wasn't such a feeling of masters and servant between them these days and she knew that she was viewed as someone who holds her position of responsibility well. Without her using such words, Zita was someone who was invaluable to the household. She managed every aspect of it and was at a point where she was so experienced at it, as it had formed the basis of most of her life now, that she had practically as much authority over it as anyone in the family.

With this excess of money that the Fatinellis always had, she decided that she was going to speak to the Signor next week to try to allocate another expenditure.

She asked to meet him on the Monday as he would be back in Pistoia on the Tuesday. They discussed the family's finances and she found out that despite his business plans not going to be as developed as he had originally expected, the family were still going to be better off.

At this point, Zita made her proposal:

"May I ask, sir, that a small amount of the income is used for an extra expenditure?"

"And what may that be?" he wondered. Up until recently, he would have dismissed it without even hearing it if he wasn't in the mood to discuss spending his money on things other than his luxuries.

"The three silver coins that you let me use to help feed the poor people in the village was very useful," she went on. He listened intently. "As you and your family are going to become wealthier still, would it be possible to put aside three coins every week for the same purpose?"

Fatinelli raised his eyebrows. It was a bold effort of anyone to ask him to give up some of his money, especially if it was to benefit outsiders. He thought about it for a moment.

"Three silver coins every week, you say?"

"If sir would allow that. I don't think it will cause any great disadvantage to your accounts or your income and the Lord would view you most favourably, of course."

He was about to accept her proposal anyway but as she informed him of the Lord's involvement in the arrangement, he knew he couldn't have refused. Maybe to another acquaintance but not to Zita.

"I think that would be fine," he answered. "I will also allow you to spend the time that you need to look after your people when you go into the village."

Zita was very grateful for this news. She thanked him heartily and told him she would be saying a special prayer for him.

This expenditure came into force immediately and Zita was glad to be able to spend a little more time with feeding her needy subjects. As time went on, she altered her plans and took food with her every morning so that she could help them more often, after she had been to church.

The practice continued for many years and Zita's authority increased with it. She soon got to the point where she treated her master and mistress as though they were her equals. They didn't put up any opposition to her principles as it was difficult to argue against the good work that she was doing. Along with this, Zita was able to command greater sums of money to be used for helping the sick and the poor. She would ask her master to bring cloth back from his trips so that she could make more clothes. The people of the village spoke of her as the lady who could save lives. It is certain that she rescued many people from impending death and many of them recovered fully from their illnesses.

By the time Zita was in her thirties, she was seen as an important leader by anyone who knew her. But she was feared by no-one. Her compassion had no limits. She had declared that she wanted to build a home where those who couldn't take care of themselves could be sheltered. There were beds for twenty people. In the beginning, Zita would be the one to take care of them. It became a great strain on her working life and, although Signor Fatinelli was willing to let her spend many hours, sometimes whole days, at the home, he felt they needed to talk.

"Zita, you are working so hard at the moment."

"Yes sir, but I enjoy every moment of it."

"I know that and I also know that God takes great care of you for being so committed."

"Thank you, sir."

"However, your tiredness is starting to show. You are only thirty-four years old but you look much older."

Her appearance did not concern Zita at all but she let him get to his point.

"What I am afraid of is that you will fall ill yourself, due to overwork, and maybe that you will die before your time."

"I will die when the Lord feels it is my time to leave this earth."

"Of course, but I think we can make that happen later rather than sooner."

"What do you mean, sir?"

"I think it would be better if you have some help in your home for the sick," he explained.

"But who could we ask to do that? I do it because it doesn't require any more money."

"I know but if I paid for one or two people to work alongside you and you trained them to do the work, you wouldn't have to be there so much and would have more time to rest. And this is what I am most concerned about."

"Really, sir? That is a wonderful idea!"

"It is merely the choice between having you pass away while you are still young and all your good work coming to an end or paying for some extra workers so that you can continue helping for longer."

Zita agreed that it was a very practical and sympathetic solution. She admitted that she was becoming more tired with her unending work.

15. Zita thought about taking on some people from Montsegradi itself. As she knew so many people very well, she chose two young women from the village who would benefit from having paid work and wouldn't have to travel to attend the home. Magdalena and Claudia spent weeks being educated about every detail necessary to know to take proper care of the people who stayed there. At first, Zita would only allow them to be present while she was there. She felt that all the responsibilities regarding the patients health was her own and she didn't want her two young recruits to be scared with their new roles. Zita explained to them how the patients should each be washed, what food they should eat and at what times, and how to act if their situations worsened.

As the two trainees became responsible employees, Zita slowly reduced her working hours at the home. Due to her passion for taking care of the people, she didn't want to be away from them. However, with time, she became more trusting and confident of the nurses and would sometimes even be prepared to miss a day when she normally visited them.

Over the years, Filipe had managed to become liberated from his feelings towards Zita. He still cared greatly for her but got married when he was twenty-seven. He and his wife moved into one of the family's smaller houses not far away and they had two children. Zita's beliefs and actions had a profound effect on him. As he had observed her carefully throughout his life, he took many of her principles with him and passed them on to his own children. He continued in the business of trade and worked alongside his father. As he was now needing to provide for his family, he was working more but due to his desire to be fair and not disadvantage his clients, he never became as rich as his father expected him to. He didn't mind; as long as he earned enough money to keep his family and his house (he only had one housekeeper), he was content to go through life with a clear conscience.

His and his siblings' families regularly visited the main Fatinelli house for dinner at weekends, so he kept contact with Zita and he was always eager to hear what she had been doing from week to week.

The home for the sick gradually developed over the years. Magdalena and Claudia became highly skilled at caring for the patients and they cooked proper meals for those who stayed there to help them recover. Not all of them could move on to live their lives independently. Those who were too old and had developed dementia could only be cared for in the home until God decided to take them away to rest eternally. Many of the patients were accepted there because they had no family, no home and no source of income. Due to being unable to feed themselves, they became weak and ill and as long as there was a free bed and there was no-one else who needed it more than they did, they were allowed to stay.

Throughout Zita's years of care and devotion, she saw patients who hadn't walked for some time regain their strength to be able to walk again. Illnesses came and went and visible ailments such as skin diseases cleared for some fortunate ones.

Zita received many compliments from people in the village and the father at the church. He told her she would be given a special place in heaven with the Lord and he viewed her as the most selfless individual he had ever known.

She, of course, respected those words but, as always, she never became proud of her achievements. In her eyes, this was simply the work that she had been assigned to do by God and as long as it pleased Him, she would be more than happy to do it until her last day on this earth.

As Zita got older, she became more careful with her own health. She wore more layers of clothing to keep her warm during the winter or at night; this had been partly encouraged by those who knew her and who also pointed out to her, like her master, that they didn't want to see her go before her time.

With her work more effectively divided between the house and the home for the sick, she was able to keep up with her tasks without becoming overworked. Her sleeping area remained the same throughout her life, in that awkward space in the attic, where most people would be ashamed to live. But that was her sanctuary; her peaceful space that only she was familiar with. It was where she could best keep regular correspondence with her saviour and this never faltered even up to the point where her health did.

She had, of course, outlived her masters, who had died when Zita was in her fifties. Giuseppe became the master of the house and lived there with his wife and their three children. By the time she was sixty years old, her many years of selfless hard work had taken her to the point where the Lord made the decision that she had done enough and it was time for to rest with Him in heaven.

It was spring 1272 and she hadn't been to the home for more than four weeks. She felt very sad that she couldn't visit the current patients. Magdalena had already died some years previously and Claudia had trained her niece to work alongside her. They missed Zita's visits, as did the patients. Many people from the village and the church came to the Fatinelli house to visit Zita when she became bedridden. Giuseppe had tried to convince her that she should stay in what was Filipe's old bed while she was ill. He said that when she recovered, she could go back to her space if she so desired. Zita thanked him but declined. She did not want anyone to have pity on her and she remained in her attic. He paid for the best medical attention to be given to her, to hopefully bring her health back so that she could do what she was put on the earth for.

However, it was not to be. She received her last sacraments and knew that she was going to leave them very soon. Her visitors couldn't help but kneel at her side in floods of tears but

Zita could still give them a smile and tell them not to worry. She was ready to meet the Lord.

Zita passed away in her sleep on the 27th of April 1272 and her loss was felt by everyone who had known her. The father held a special service for her funeral and almost everybody in the surrounding area attended.

Zita was buried in the cemetery of St. Frediano's church. The people were in mourning for her for many months. Some felt like they'd lost a part of themselves and mourned for the rest of their lives.

She lay in the cemetery for over three hundred years before renovations meant that the graves needed to be dug and skeletons had to be relocated with their tombstones. It was 1580 when Zita's grave was exhumed. She was found to be in her complete physical state. Even though she had not been embalmed at the time of her death, she still had all her skin. Pope Leo X granted her an office in her honour. Zita was canonised as a saint in 1696 and is the patron saint of maids and domestic servants.

Zita's body was later mummified and placed in a glass coffin to be displayed inside the basilica of San Frediano in Lucca, Italy where she can still be seen today, more than seven hundred years after her death.

Author's note:

I chose to write this story as I spent a short time living in Lucca and visited the mentioned basilica. I found it astonishing to know that Saint Zita's body had survived for so long in an incorrupt state. Some years later, when remembering about Zita, I was interested to know her story. I found that there were a few church records that gave a basic outline of her life and two stories had been written but were no longer in print. So I used the information that I could find to create this story. I hope that I have written one that the readers will think is a suitable work of fiction for this most altruistic lady.

Elliot Lord, 2011

Printed in Great Britain
by Amazon